To Ad
Bob Krusadu,

Thank you good sir
for all that you do to
create beauty and
amplify the wonderful
experience that is Athens.

SILENCE
William M. Brandon III

I am
pleased to
know you sir!

This book is a work of fiction. Names, characters, places and incidents are products of the author's imagination or are used fictitiously. Any resemblance to actual events or locales or persons, living or dead, is entirely coincidental.

Copyright © 2000 & 2014 by William M. Brandon III

All rights reserved, including the right to reproduce this book or portions thereof in any form whatsoever. For further information, please contact: info@blackhillpress.com

ISBN-13: 978-0615962047
ISBN-10: 0615962041

Edited by Elise Portale
Artwork by Davide Bonazzi

Printed in the U.S.A.

BLACK HILL PRESS
blackhillpress.com

Black Hill Press is a publishing collective founded on collaboration. Our growing family of writers and artists are dedicated to the novella—a distinctive, often overlooked literary form that offers the focus of a short story and the scope of a novel. We believe a great story is never defined by its length.

Our independent press produces uniquely curated collections of Contemporary American Novellas. We also celebrate innovative paperback projects with our Special Editions series. Books are available in both print and digital formats, online and in your local bookstore, library, museum, university gift shop, and selected specialty accounts. Discounts are available for book clubs and teachers.

Contemporary American Novellas
1. Corrie Greathouse, *Another Name for Autumn*
2. Ryan Gattis, *The Big Drop: Homecoming*
3. Jon Frechette, *The Frontman*
4. Richard Gaffin, *Oneironautics*
5. Ryan Gattis, *The Big Drop: Impermanence*
6. Alex Sargeant, *Sci-Fidelity*
7. Veronica Bane, *Mara*
8. Kevin Staniec, *Begin*
9. Arianna Basco, *Palms Up*
10. Douglas Cowie, *Sing for Life: Tin Pan Alley*
11. Tomas Moniz, *Bellies and Buffalos*
12. Brett Arnold, *Avalon, Avalon*
13. Douglas Cowie, *Sing for Life: Away, You Rolling River*

14. Pam Jones, *The Biggest Little Bird*
15. Peppur Chambers, *Harlem's Awakening*
16. Kate St. Clair, *Spelled*
17. Veronica Bane, *Miyuki*
18. William Brandon, *Silence*

<u>Special Editions</u>
1. Kevin Staniec, *29 to 31: A Book of Dreams*

for
William Jr.
Rachel Anne
&
Shirley Catherine

Unique and incredibly special thanks to my astonishing wife Crystal and the wee brilliant little man, Sir Quentin. Without their support and inspiration none of the preceding, current, or following would have been possible.

I love you both dearly.

Severing Ties

One minute, fifty seconds. Hurry up guys, please, hurry up.

It was a dry, bright day in Los Angeles and the intersection of Sunset and Vine was dense with movement.

The threat of imminent extinction brought on by fear of a computational catastrophe at the turn of the century had slightly dampened America's feeling of invincibility. The movement of the moment had the inhabitants of Los Angeles dressing down to look like the residents of Seattle, but no matter how you pitched it to the marketing team, Los Angeles was no place for flannel shirts and knit caps. Watching Los Angelinos trudge through their sun-beaten streets wearing enough wool to ward off a Pacific Northwest squall never ceased to amuse me. Sad, and indicative, really.

A patrol car turned right onto Vine from Leland Way and moved slowly through the intersection. The officers were primarily concerned with the length of skirts on that warm afternoon and were unimpressed by a man in a pinstripe suit standing outside of a bank and eying them up.

They were driving far too casually to be responding to a bank alarm, so when they veered left at Hollywood Boulevard, I returned to watching the street.

Five seconds. They should have already wrapped this up. I wonder if . . .

Gunshot.

Oh, Christ, this is it. I stepped inside the bank to witness the boys mowing down everyone in sight. Rich crimson arcs painted the walls and teller windows, bodies lay in broken heaps across the long marble foyer, gunsmoke burned the air. I stepped back outside and cocked my 9mm. I am the point man. I see all things at all times. This was my part in the insidious plan.

Today, everything had gone horribly wrong. The boys made a pact before we had begun pulling gigs together that if one civilian got shot, every civilian died. Once someone got capped, it was no longer just a bank robbery; it become murder one. There could be no witnesses. The pact had always struck me as a *tough guy* posture . . . now, I knew better. We had bigger problems now. Stretch was approaching in the car, *right on time*.

"Let's GO. GO, GO, GO!"

Into the car, the force of acceleration made it impossible to fasten my safety restraint right away.

"What happened, what caused all the chaos?" I looked around the car.

"Some John Wayne motherfucker went for the alarm, so I dealt with him. What was I supposed to do? If it's between us going to prison and some worthless rent-a-cop getting waxed, I say *bon voyage, Tubby*." Mike was the type whose finger was poised on the trigger because he was dying for a reason to squeeze.

"Shut the fuck up. We're not in the clear yet. You ladies sit back and try to look like the rest of the zombies in this city. Got it?" Jake was our efficient and somewhat unstable head honcho. The phrase *nerves of steel* never had a clear-cut definition until Jake walked the Earth.

We drove down Sunset Boulevard to UCLA and ditched the getaway car in parking structure seven. We continued from there in four different vehicles—north, south, east, and west. I traveled south on the 405 Freeway in my black and beaten 51' Mercury. I must have smoked an entire pack of Pall Malls on the way to Costa Mesa. The world was spinning, and a sudden realization struck me: I was responsible for the deaths of twenty innocent people. I was barely old enough to hold a master's degree and I had already stolen millions. I wondered if the money I would receive in three weeks would compensate for the guilt. The dead slap of limp bodies against the bank floor and the ping of ricocheting bullets drove all other sounds from my mind. I loosened my necktie in hopes that this oppression would subside. It didn't—my pinstripe suit was a felonious precursor.

The 405 started backing up around Long Beach, so I slipped down to PCH. It was my third gig with the boys, and I wondered when it would be enough. We were already monetarily set for life, but with our profession came an addiction to the rush. Money is the most important thing in the world; people died every day protecting it, and we got our kicks punching holes in their fortified walls. But my blood was beginning to thin after the fiasco I had just witnessed. Was I losing my edge? Possibly . . . probably. Maybe I should pack it up and head out to Vegas where I belong. What if we were all thinking the same damn thing, but none of us had the guts to say a word?

Exactly three weeks later, I strutted into the Knight at the brazenly early hour of 10:00 p.m. with a fresh shave, fresh haircut, and a new suit. When I walked in, the boys were seated at our booth in the back. Our trademark cloud of cigarette and cigar smoke obscured my vision of Mike, Jake, and Stretch. The cramped, sodden walls and carpeting yawned apathy and none of the lost souls hugging the rail turned from their drinks. I walked up to the bar, gave Tony the Barkeep a firm handshake, and ordered a beer.

"Where ya been Dean-o?" Tony's haphazard beach-bum ponytail whipped as he turned.

"You know, here and there. It's good to see you, Tony. So, what do you charge for a beer these days?"

"It's on the house, Dean-o. It's good to have the boys back in the old dive. You hear about those hoods that robbed that piggy bank in L.A.?" Tony gestured to the television hanging over the end of the bar. News of the robbery was still being replayed on the midday programs when the news cycle was slow. "Got away with a few million, scot-free. Lucky fucks."

"On the house you say? Make that straight gin. Wait, make that a double."

"You're a real bastard, Dean." Tony smiled.

"That's what I hear, Tony . . . that's what I hear."

I joined the boys at the booth, exchanged how-do-you-dos, and had a seat.

"What's shakin', Dean?" Mike looked me up and down.

"Not much. Layin' low."

Mike knew something was up; I needed to relax and stop thinking about all of those dead people. It made me nervous that I knew next to nothing about Mike—especially since he outed himself as trigger-happy. He came in on Jake's say-so. I trusted Jake; we had busted a few noses together as bouncers in Hollywood several years back. It had all been Jake's idea: the robberies, the crews, the targets. He had ten years on me and had done some time at San Quentin. He said he *knew people*, and I believed him. And this job was the perfect job: Getting off at 2:00 a.m. meant I couldn't waste my pay at the bar. I brought Stretch into the crew. His daddy grew up in Marion County, Alabama, just 103 miles from Birmingham. Driving fast was what Stretch was born to do.

We sat around and had a bullshit session for about an hour, Mike seemed to relax a bit, then Jake rapped his knuckles on the table to commence the meeting.

"Okay, everyone's here, let's get down to business. Everyone's cut is settled. Dean, yours is in a locker at LAX— here's the key and number. Mike, yours is in a post office box in Santa Ana—here's the key and number. Stretch, yours is in a locker at Ports O'Call in San Pedro—here's the number and key. Gentlemen, job well done. Sources say the police have no leads, except eyewitness accounts that four men in pinstripe suits and black masks sped away in a beaten up '52 Chevy. Lucky for us, it's the '90s and every idiot Ska fan in Orange County owns a pinstripe suit."

"No descriptions?"

"White male, 5'10 to 6'2", dark hair, blue eyes, sketchy looking skinny kid up to no good." Jake laughed and slapped me on the back.

"That sounds about right." Stretch chimed in.

"No descriptions, good." This relieved me because, as point man, I don't wear a mask. Looks a little suspicious—man standing outside a bank in a black mask. If anyone were going to be fingered by a description, it would be my paranoid ass. I felt a soft hand on my shoulder.

"Are you Jake?"

It had been a while since I had heard a voice that sultry. Jake stood up.

"That would be me. Ladies, please have a seat." Jake leaned over to me, "Two-grand a piece, but worth every penny."

"Whores, Jake? I swear your libido has no discerning thought process."

Mike and Stretch leaned in like kids at the peep show. Unfortunately for them, Jake had intended the second girl for me; he had no intention of sharing with anyone else.

I finished my drink and said, "Gentlemen . . . ladies, it's been a lovely evening, but I'm swinging out early."

"Where the hell are you going?"

"Easy Jake; I'm meeting someone. Besides, you know tricks aren't my style."

"All right, man. I'll catch you later. The plan still holds. Barring tonight, keep a low profile for three more weeks. Got that, ya jerks?"

The stunning brunette who had situated herself next to me grabbed my hand and asked me to stay.

"I'm sorry, ladies, not my cup of tea."

With that said, I glided to my Mercury and disappeared into the coastal mist.

On the subject of worthwhile expenditures of time, I had been waiting for an hour overlooking the cliffs at Point Fermin and it looked like Helen wasn't going to show. Once again, I sat waiting, holding vigil for someone who let me down. I stretched out on the barrier wall and watched the stars struggle to penetrate the city light with their million-year-old beauty. I remembered how clearly you could see the stars on the road to Las Vegas. I thought about my absent lady friend. The young lady I had discussed galaxies with, enveloped in the warmth of a blazing fire. Helen was so alive, so desirable. When she was in my arms, I felt I could convince her to leave her man and run away with me to Vegas. We could gaze into the onyx sky and discuss the universe as if it were in the room with us. But I said nothing of what I felt and He was still holding her. If only I could say all the words I desired to, if only my tongue wasn't bound by incriminating shyness. I would have told her not to beat herself in the head over a decision that is best made by her heart. But I am not that brave, and besides, I couldn't, in good conscience, bring such a lovely young woman into my world.

That night clinched it.

I had nothing left. The next morning, I put on my black suit, white shirt, black suspenders, my black wingtips, and a fire-engine-red tie from the vault of a 1940's tailor. I was ready for Vegas. I stepped out the front door with one suitcase and a black hat. I took one final look around my apartment and left.

Jake was walking up my street and leaned on the hood of my car.

"Was comin' by to see how you were holding up. You seemed pretty edgy last night—even for you. Where ya headed, Dean-o?"

"Vegas."

"How long will you be gone?"

"I don't know, probably forever."

"What will the boys do without their point man?"

"I'm through Jake. That last gig in L.A. gave me the creeps, and I'm pulling out. I've got enough dough to write for the rest of my life—or drink myself into oblivion, whichever comes first. Besides, you know I'm far too paranoid to keep going after I get that *feeling* about gigs."

"It pains me to see you go. I thought I'd always have the Deanster covering my ass, but if it's what you have to do . . . How about havin' a beer with me before you jet?"

"Anything for you, Jake."

As is always the case, we ended up at the Knight. The density of sorrow trapped behind the Knight's heavy back door was greater during daylight hours—much darker in spite of sad strands of sunlight wresting through old windows whose black overcoat had chipped.

"I can't believe you're taking off." Jake broke a long silence.

"Sure you can. You know I lose when I gamble. Always have."

"You gambled on me, man," Jake responded.

"More like you gambled on me," I reminded him.

Jake thought I was a chump at first glance: skinny, never had a broken nose, did my job without much talking. One night while working together in Hollywood, I carded an aging rockstar's date. She didn't have ID, so I refused to let her in. The situation escalated into a shouting match. When the rockstar's bodyguard took a swing at me, I moved easily and broke his nose. When the rest of the rockstar's entourage circled around me, Jake backed my play. The rockstar called off his security detail and they left en masse to patronize another Hollywood hotspot. Jake patted me on the shoulder, *Nice work, kid. Didn't know you had it in ya.* Truth was, I didn't; I'd never started a fight, but I had been finishing fights all of my life.

"Besides, Jake, you pitched a solid plan, and with the exception of that last job in L.A., it was always easy money." I had no complaints.

"That's why I picked you. You're a nervous wreck about every single detail, but when its time to go, your mind shuts off and you react. Look. I need you on this crew. Replacing you will mean rethinking the process. Any chance you'll stay?"

"No chance."

The L.A. gig hadn't shaken Jake loose. I was the only one seeing screaming faces in my peripheral vision.

"When are you going to pull up and call it quits?" I wanted to know.

"Right before my luck runs out." Jake forced a smile.

§

I never saw Jake again. Gunshot wound to the stomach. Some rent-a-cop tagged him as he was backing out the door with a measly twenty grand on a solo gig. He bled to death on an anonymous sidewalk.

Here I go, 110 mph down Interstate 15, Pall Mall in one hand, my lucky silver whiskey flask in the other, and my trusty left knee doing all the steering. It wasn't long before I lost the shirt and drained the flask. I could not wait to feel the 100-percent moisture-free, oppressive desert heat. For some inane reason, there was a traffic jam halfway out of Victorville, so I slipped out to Route 66 and took the nostalgic highway to Barstow. It always made the trip so much more interesting. Deadbeat Barstow evaporated in my rearview mirror and I was finally ahead of the weekend rush headed for the distant desert Gomorrah.

I was parched by the time I reached Baker, but there was no time to stop; I had to keep going. I had just enough gas to reach the Strip and I meant to keep driving until I did. The metal-crested buildings of the Baker Correctional Facility reflected the intense high-desert sunlight as I climbed the hill. The large cluster of one-story, reinforced buildings sat sentry at the gaping maw of Death Valley. The slow crawl out of Baker has knocked scores of cars out of commission over the years; I patted my dashboard and congratulated the car for making the climb look like slow stroll in the park.

When I reached the stateline, I felt a very intense sense of urgency to start fresh, to begin again. A new chapter for Dean O'Leary. New lives, new adventures, and most of all, more money than I could ever possibly spend. Time to breath, to write—or at least attempt to. I still clung to a precious few delusions to keep me warm at night. As I crested the edge of the Vegas valley, I thought to myself, *Yeah man, you're finally going to be happy.*

Gnawing Cold

It happened in late October. When else does love strike with such potency? The wind is bitter; the Vegas floor is cracked with the pain of extreme cold and a wretched dislike for moisture. The modern sands of The Meadows separate and bleed the cries of centuries marred by bitter, tasteless decadence and primitive hedonism. The Earth-bound knuckle has long since passed, but even at the end of the twentieth century, Cro-Magnon mentality still expels its venomous odor into Vegas's neon palaces and envelops those who dare tread where addictions run deeper than steel needles under Tangiers' stars.

The desert's signature wind-chill factor gnawed at my joints, making me fear life past forty (though I have never thought of life past thirty as anything but the inevitable deterioration of all that is precious—all that is matter).

These bitter winds swept my darling Audene across deserts and into my tragedy. The incision was made in six weeks' time—from my first glance at her beauty until the day

I would see her no more. We stood side by side, inhaling carcinogens outside of The Plaza Hotel—she was a vision. Her calm, light skin glowed naturally beneath her dark, subtle eyes, and her delicate nose was peppered with youthful freckles. She wore no makeup and, from where I was standing, looked like she had never needed to. Her short, mousey brown hair was kept hidden beneath a soft knit cap that covered her head like a big-sister hand-me-down. There was no façade about her, only a brutal and sad truth that she seemed to keep at bay just below the surface. Audene was not a woman who would cause legions to wage war but a woman whose eyes told of the pain that such spontaneous men of ignorance left in their wake. A woman who had been murdered by another's passion. She felt the pain I felt but without my tempered logic.

We began speaking to each other strangely, unlike the beginning of any acquaintance: I, quite by accident, stepped on her wonderfully delicate feet and she instinctively delivered a shot to my midriff that sent me stumbling. Such intensity should never have been hidden behind such cold, earth-colored eyes. But who was I to deny the beauty of Gaia as a disguise for ill-tempered logic and razor-sharp instincts?

"Nice shot."

"Fuck off." She never looked up.

"What's your name?"

"Look, I said . . . "

"*Fuck off*, yeah, I know. I asked you another question." When she lifted her head, I smiled. "I'm Dean."

"Nice to meet you, Dean." She didn't return my smile.

She was like a serpent that finds its spine against an impenetrable barrier. Striking out is the only option and death of opposition is the only acceptable end result. We returned to silence, but I couldn't leave it alone.

"Have a nice evening." I crushed the remains of my cigarette against the sole of my shoe and tossed it in a long arc into a nearby advertisement-littered trash bin.

"Audene. My name's Audene." She offered her hand to me; her long fingers wrapped pensively around my hand but seemed to relax and enjoy the warmth of the embrace. She pulled her hand away after a long moment and tucked it back into her long navy coat as if the entire episode had never happened.

"It's a pleasure. Mind having a drink with me?"

She thought about it for a moment and then relented stoically, "Sure. Why not?"

We left Fremont and ducked into a proper dive on East Stewart.

"I come here when the din of slot machines bells becomes too much to endure."

She smiled. She understood.

"It's always nice to see that people still appreciate Downtown."

"The Strip is Disneyland," she replied quietly.

"Indeed." *Well put my fair lady, well put.* "What would you like to drink?" The barkeep approached apathetically. By his wobbling gait, I'd guess he'd taken a shot in a foreign war circa 1950. He stood silently waiting for us to order.

"Jameson neat and a shot of Johnnie Black."

Quite an order. "Sapphire and tonic. I'll join her on the shot."

The bartender left to mix and Audene lit a long, white cigarette. "You really should watch where you are walking."

I smiled. "Yes, I should. Although, who knows, maybe stepping on your toe was the best mistake I've made in a long time."

She looked at me with playful suspicion. She seemed to be struggling, *is this guy for real*?

"I'm going to take a stab in the dark and guess that you aren't from Las Vegas." I wanted to keep the momentum . . .

"Good guess. Then again, is anyone from Vegas . . . "

The bartender placed our drinks down sloppily and got uncomfortably close to Audene's face.

"If you two are here on a *date*, finish up your drinks and beat it."

"Fuck you, you inbred sister-fucker!" Audene shrieked and threw her neat Irish whiskey in the barkeep's face.

I leapt to my feet, not sure if I should restrain Audene or hit the bartender for whatever he said that had offended her. I chose the former. I left a twenty on the bar and walked Audene out the back door.

"Hey, are you okay?"

"Yes." She wasn't very convincing. "He thought I was a prostitute."

"Oh." That made more sense. "Oh," it occurred to me a little late: He thought I was the John. "I should have taken a pop at him."

She smiled. "Complete asshole."

I was fascinated by her dismissive strength; we began a long walk amidst Las Vegas's former epicenter. Our journey terminated in the lobby of the Golden Gate Café, where I offered her an early breakfast.

"I should really be going." Her clear cinnamon eyes retreated and began to scan the ground for some sort of escape hatch.

"Of course," I was confused by her desperation to leave. "I'd like to see you again . . ."

"Tomorrow. Same time; I'll take you up on that breakfast offer."

"Perfect." I stepped toward her to offer a parting hug. She swam into my arms and held tightly, as a child holds their totem blanket. She seemed to realize how tightly she was holding and backed away, looking into my eyes plaintively.

"It must be incredible to make love to you," was all she said.

I didn't know what to say. Aside from confusion, I wondered if the edges of terror were apparent in my stare. There was something about Audene that I didn't want to know.

She handed me a torn slip of thick ivory typing paper. Its pristine surface marred only by blue ink: her number scribbled in mad tension and anxiety. Audene turned on her heel and silently walked away.

I was suspicious—I was afraid for my heart—I was afraid for my life—I was afraid for my mind—but as I watched her strut out of the door, I knew I could not walk away, not now. I watched as she pulled a soft wool cap over her short, chaotic hair. She waved over her shoulder without turning and disappeared into the darkness.

The next time I saw Audene, we ate lunch at the same spot, and she asked me to marry her. I was shocked. She didn't even know my last name. I kissed her for the first time, and it was terribly confusing. I simultaneously felt elation beyond my expectations and a fear in the back of my mind that this woman was somehow manipulating my emotions—unrecognizable to the naked eye. I lost this moment when she kissed me again.

"Yes, yes, I will."

For the very first time, I saw her smile, truly smile. It broke through the storm cloud of chagrin, and I saw what I had only hypothesized about . . . happiness. I brought this woman happiness. I could see it in her eyes, when I touched her, when she laid her head on my chest. Something about me seemed to make her complete.

Now, I was petrified. I had said 'yes' to her proposal with an extreme degree of flippancy, but she was dead serious, perhaps as serious as she had ever been in her entire life—but how? How could she know me enough to be that certain over the course of three days? I felt enormous walls shooting up all around me; I was at the bottom of a cavernous trap looking up at the receding sun. I felt helpless to even check the walls to see if they were scalable. This is wrong . . . this is wrong . . . this is wrong.

This admission frayed my sense of peace. I was determined to prove that someone loving me as irrationally as Audene did could be enough. I had stumbled on and been slowly bled to death by my own romantic barbs. Chasing again and again a moment that never comes. *I will love Audene as she loves me—one day.*

Slowly, I became more frightened of her frenzy, her compulsiveness, and her obsession with me. I wrote this off as cold feet, and we continued to plan the big day.

My pensive bride was fighting a silent war against a fetish for inhaling elaborate chemicals into her nasal passages—creating the frame for her portrait of agony. This is the battle without end, a war with no victors.

"Tell me something no one else knows." Audene looked up at me from her resting position on my chest.

"Hm." There were so many things, most of which would probably never grace my lips again. "I was actually born in this nightmare of a town. Born but not raised."

"Where were you raised?" she asked, rolling on to her side and running languid fingers down my thigh.

"Pick a state."

"Utah." She tried a tough one first.

"Yep. Second through fourth grade. Orem, Provo, and Ogden."

"What? Seriously?"

"My family had a steadfast rule. If a place sucks, get the hell out. Pops never hesitated to pick a new place with cheaper rent and new faces."

"Virginia," she giggled.

"Yes ma'am," I smiled and kissed her forehead. "Your turn."

"No one knows much about me, so take your pick."

"Where are you from, lovely lady?"

"It's embarrassing." She looked away.

"Nonsense, I was born in this nutso town. Hit me with it."

"Bakersfield. Born and raised." Audene whispered it, like a confession.

"I've driven through. On the way to Vegas, as a matter of fact," I smiled. There was certainly something else to the story, but I wasn't positive that I wanted to press the issue.

"Dean," she sat up on the bed. "I was basically homeless when we met. I came out here to escape Bakersfield, to escape my life and my . . . "

"Mistakes," I offered.

"Maybe. I love you. Loving me, if you do, probably won't be easy. If it turns out that you don't love me, just . . . be honest, OK?"

The conversation had certainly taken an unexpected turn.

"At all times." Except right now.

Whatever she was running from when I found her was gaining on her. Our lazy days of post-nuptial celebration were interrupted abruptly.

"I have to run an errand." Audene stood over me, fully clothed with her bag clutched in both hands. "I'll be back in an hour."

"Um, OK. You have to go right now?"

"Yes." Audene kissed me slowly on the forehead. "I'll be back soon."

It was the first of many *errands*. When I could no longer accept her excuses, I followed her. I tailed her to the Northside, where she entered a small, decayed neighborhood speckled with grey, near-demolished homes. Prostitutes and Johns clogged the sidewalks, and as we sank deeper into the melee, I began to rethink my decision to follow her . . . and mistrust my desire to *know*.

Audene stopped in front of a dreary, two-story apartment building and disappeared into the ground floor. I parked and walked across the street. I sat casually on the apartment building's front step and watched Audene knock on the door for apartment A. A stout, olive-skinned man opened the door and beckoned for her to step inside.

"Kid!" I called out an adolescent on a bike.

"What?" He was not pleased about being flagged down.

"You live around here?"

"Yeah. Why?" The kid had better things to do.

"I nicked someone's car while I was parking. I want to give them my insurance info. I think he lives in apartment A; short guy, jet black hair . . ."

"Dmitri?"

Perfect, the kid gave him up.

" . . . but Dmitri's car isn't parked out here . . . "

"Thanks, kid," I waved as I returned to my car.

She returned twenty minutes later, emerged harried, wide-eyed, and anxious. She looked up and down the sidewalk several times: both ways, as if she were about to cross a highway. She seemed stuck, she could not decide to take the first step; somehow, it was too much for her to bear. She looked about once more in desperation before plopping down on a step and sobbing quietly. When tears ceased streaking her cheeks, she wiped her face, stood, and drove away.

Dmitri closed and locked his front door. I'd nearly given up on the bastard leaving his cave. His side window was easy enough to pry open, and in North Vegas, prying open a window is, well, of less *concern* than the crimes happening block by block in every direction. Dmitri's hovel was sodden with the debris of lethargy: half-consumed fast food, clothing representing various levels of cleanliness, and the reason for Audene's visit—a tiny crystallized mound of amphetamine.

I destroyed the room. I expected to feel rage, but I was consumed by one thought, *end this now.*

Her pain was only temporarily numbed by her addiction; the rage she kept subjective grew with each dose, each inhalation, each unkind word between us. My wife began disappearing more often and for longer periods of time. By the time I had given in to apathy, she would leave abruptly and not return for days at a time. When she did return, she was sullen and eager to lash out. We began communicating only at the top of our lungs. Our pain swelled together and as a result of one another.

I walked into our apartment late on a Tuesday evening. I thought she was *out*, as usual. The apartment was dark, and although I could smell their sweet aroma, all of the candles had also been put out. As I crossed the threshold and hung up my coat and hat, a sense of foreboding came over me. Death was with me in the room; it caressed the hairs on my neck. Where was she—my pain and my torture?

I felt the wind whip past my face before I heard the crack of my 9mm or smelled the burnt powder. I fell backwards to the floor and gazed blindly into the darkness. A second bullet pierced my right shoulder. There she was. I lunged toward her and wrapped my hands around hers. I gained control of my weapon and stood silent and stoic with my arm stretched taunt, the barrel pressed firmly to her forehead. I flipped a nearby switch and saw my broken Audene. I wanted to hold her, forgive her, and let her finish me off bite by bite. I saw a tear run down her cheek and mingle delicately with the destructive white powder that laced her nose and lips. I felt a warm tear spill over my eyelash and off the edge of my lips.

"It is better this way. You don't love me. Set me free . . . please." She held my hand in place and pushed my index finger against the trigger.

She was dead. I didn't try to stop her—she slumped over onto the floor face down—I was never able to stop her.

There's a small silver rock in the desert near Hesperia that I cast my shadow over once a year. I beg forgiveness and sprinkle the fine white dust—which almost killed me and delivered my wife into the ground—over the severed earth. Like my love's destroyed mind, this land takes the powder and devours it as a child devours his mother's milk. No remorse . . . only hunger.

The End of Reality as We Know It

I first saw Gaelin in a hole-in-the-wall restaurant on Sahara. The Cuban cuisine was only mediocre, but there was an awe-inspiring painting above booth 13 that very abstractly depicted the Bolshevik Revolution. I loved to sit for hours, sipping extraordinary whiskey until the hues swirled together and my numbing visage compelled me to make my escape. The paint leapt from the canvas and forced passion and guilt and pain and hope coursing through your body with such intensity that you were forced to gasp to remain a recipient of oxygen. On this eve, I heard a familiar gasp. A young man with chaotic dark hair and deep mahogany eyes behind thin spectacles was peering over my head at this painting, and I could tell by the look in his eyes that he saw what I did. He felt the magnitude of the artist's emotion. I gave a nod of appreciation for what he was feeling, saying telepathically, *I know, I understand.*

The blistering desert heat had thrust the mercury to a slow simmer at 110 degrees, and our father Sol was punishing me for my decades-late flair for style. I guess it's my fault, but there's something terribly romantic and integral about strutting into a lounge in a Las Vegas hotel smelling of whiskey and carcinogens, wrapped in a suit your grandfather had tailor-made in 1948. I was past the point of inebriation as I lit a Pall Mall and ducked into the Golden Nugget. I suddenly felt like raising a little hell at the wee hour of three o'clock in the afternoon. I wrestled a stool into position and let the cool air, sultry jazz, lack of light, and a frigid glass of gin erase my memory of the oppressive heat. Some puppet on the television was reporting a story about three chaps in San Diego that pulled off a multi-million-dollar bank heist and disappeared, literally.

"Hello, Jake. Looks like your luck is still holding up," I muttered under my breath.

As soon as the words rolled off my tongue, I heard *Starvation, and not evil, is the parent of modern crime* in my right ear. I rose from my position, hunched over yet another blessed glass of gin, to see who in this mindless lounge had quoted the flamboyant Oscar Wilde.

What I saw was supernatural. Soft ebony curls framed her gleaming emerald eyes; looking past these oceans of placid beauty would be a crime against one's self. Her velvet lips quivered slightly, as if she were on the verge of explaining to me everything poignant in this world but didn't want to take the chance that I didn't care. I was absolutely stunned, and for one brief, shining, moment, I cared. I needed to know what went on behind the glassy expanse of her jade eyes. This was the type of moment we all wish we could seal in a bottle and cast out to sea, returning endlessly with the tide to remind us that death is a truly tragic end to the lavish experience that is life.

This is where I cry.

This is where my mistress alcohol rears her jealous head and lashes my tongue until it is subservient and ambiguous. All I could squeak out was, "You're incredible."

This goddess peered into my tortured eyes, tenderly searching for the right words to say.

"I'd like to know you, but not like this," was all she said.

She kissed my cheek and it burned with subtle passion and a very vivid fear that we had simply crossed paths at the wrong time. I destroyed the beauty we should have shared together in the space of sixty seconds. As she slipped away, I turned back to my glass and traced *that's tragedy* in the condensation on the bar.

Three hours flew by and my need to be left alone with my mistress was intensifying. Drinking alone was my last resort, but solitude and alcohol called to me in unison all too often.

"Make it a screwdriver this time, barkeep." I needed my spirits lifted. The drink came and I lamented letting her go without a fight; my loss of her is a pain I shall always deny.

The next time I saw Gaelin, I was playing poker in Caesar's Palace when a hand came to rest on my shoulder.

"Hello, friend." It was the mysterious art lover. I gestured for him to take the seat next to me. I was too drunk to notice that there was already someone sitting there.

"Beat it, pal," were the first words out of my mouth. I assume I said this with conviction because the man picked up his chips and left.

"I'm Dean. Who are you?" My manners tend to diminish when I'm going on my fifth hour of drinking and gambling.

"It's a pleasure to make your acquaintance. I'm Gaelin." His strictly late-'90s attire and prescription spectacles made us an odd pair, but it was Vegas: *odd* has a higher standard.

"What brings you to Vegas?"

"I live here. I've always been a hedonist at heart, and when the rest of my body caught up, I ended up here. What about you? You look like you just rolled out of a Lon Chaney film."

"It's an incredibly long, involved story of self-loathing, not acceptable for the opening of a friendship. I'll admit, I'm not sure if I should shake your hand or pistol-whip you. I get the feeling there's more to our meeting than simple camaraderie."

"Do you believe in fate?"

"Not even a little bit," I retorted. "I do have a highly developed tendency to walk blindly into dangerous situations. I just haven't decided if you qualify as dangerous."

As a gesture of faith, Gaelin bet $1,000 on the next hand. Cards slid swiftly to land within his gaze. He peered at his hand and gave no sign of victory or defeat. The dealer smiled, as he did at every hand, and arrogantly tapped the rail. He stared at Gaelin, challenging him to keep raising.

As the betting closed, Gaelin laid down his cards.

"Full house, number of the Beast over kings."

The dealer had three aces.

"Well, well, Dean," Gaelin smiled, "fate is apparently on our side. Where to next?"

The Necessity of Adversity I

Jesus, it's cold. Gaelin and I walked out of the casino into the frigid desert night. The Strip lay glowing before us — actually, for me, it was more fuzzy than glowing. Seven hours of drinking and gambling had really put a damper on my sense of sight. I staggered a bit and began falling toward oncoming traffic. In the blink of an eye, Gaelin had his arm around my waist and had restored me to an upright position.

"You're a real bastard when you're drunk, you know that?"

"That's what I hear, that's what I . . . " I stopped for a moment. Call it the one and only moment of clarity I've ever had. Everyone I have cared enough about to speak more than two sentences to had said something to that effect. Most said a lot more. Was I in trouble? Did I dominate my mistress alcohol, or was I the bound and gagged recipient of her lashings? Why did it matter? I went to the bottle because I wanted to, because she made me forget, because I loved her, because I needed to — damn.

"Are you OK? Looks like I'm losing you," Gaelin queried.

"Yeah, I'm fine. I'm just working through some things with my head. We fight a lot, especially when we're drunk."

"Let's grab something to eat. My treat—the last three hands paid exceptionally," Gaelin offered.

"How much did you make?" At least one of us was accomplishing more than getting drunk.

"About ten grand after the dealer's tip."

"How much did you tip him?"

"A grand."

"You gave that jackass a thousand dollars for doing his job?" I couldn't believe it.

"Trust me, he earned it."

"How do you figure?"

"Let's just say that when you have a reputation as a big tipper, certain things are revealed to you." Gaelin lowered his voice.

"Like what?"

"Nothing concrete, just a change in attitude, or position. A slight change in facial gestures lets you know when to bet big and when to lie low."

"You mean they cheat for you?"

"Not entirely. They're dealing the cards the exact same way, but dealers develop the ability to count cards. They know all of the probabilities; it's their job. So they have instincts like any other gambler, perhaps a little more based in scientific fact, but instincts nonetheless. When sweet cards are swinging around, they'll let me know."

I had completely underestimated Gaelin; I didn't usually make that mistake.

"So that full house was a hint?"

"No, that guy's a straight shooter, he doesn't fool around. That's why I smiled like such an asshole as he handed me my chips. He's a tough guy to beat, which is why I suggested we move to another table after I took him for that last three grand."

"You're a sly one, all right. So, what sounds good for eats?"

"I don't know, how about—oh shit."

"What's the matter?" I felt the cold barrel of a handgun on my neck. "Oh shit."

We were ushered into a side alley near a service entrance for a casino. I was slammed into a wall face first and a second man held Gaelin at gunpoint.

"Where's your cash, asshole?" grunted the first man.

"What do you mean?" Gaelin asked unconvincingly.

The first man pulled the hammer back. "Don't fuck with me. I have a firearm pressed firmly against your neck. If I sneeze, you lose your head and I find the money on your dead body anyway. It's your choice."

I interjected: "Looks like neither of you have a silencer handy. We are approximately fifteen feet away from prying ears, perhaps even a cop. Not to mention about twenty cooks and busboys right inside this door." I rapped on the metal door. "Do you want to walk out of this alley as free men, or do you want to spend the rest of your already quite sad life wondering if your grip on the soap is tight enough? It's *your* choice."

I couldn't believe the way I was talking to this hoodlum. I can't dodge bullets any more than the next guy. There was a long pause; I think he agreed with my logic. The barrel left my neck, and I heard the air moving around the gun as it struck the back of my head.

Darkness . . .

My head hurt like the night I abused a lethal amount of Goldschläger and ended up in the middle of the desert firing a 9mm into the darkness. I sat up and took a look around. Gaelin was on the ground next to me. I checked his pulse. He was alive, but if he felt anything like I did, he'd wish he wasn't. Everything looked dirtier to me for some reason. Almost dying at the hands of amateur thugs puts a tint of filth on the world that one doesn't recognize until they've fallen victim. I slapped Gaelin's face.

"Wake up. They're gone. We must have been unconscious all night—it's 1:00 p.m. already."

"At least we're not dead," Gaelin responded groggily.

"Well, I have ten bucks, do you still want breakfast? Well, scratch that. Looks like they found my ten bucks." My pockets were empty.

"Don't worry about it—those punks didn't get my money."

"They didn't?"

"Hell, no. The casino cuts a check. I have a tab going at the Golden Gate Café; breakfast is on me."

It was obvious that nothing had changed about the Golden Gate Café in forty years. When something's not broken, don't bother trying to fix it.

Our server arrived, pad in hand and pen poised.

"What can I get for you gentlemen?"

"Steak and eggs, well done," I answered.

"Ditto, make mine medium rare."

"Say, is Jennifer working today?"

"Sorry, I don't know of a Jennifer working here." The waitress looked at me, confused.

"She worked yesterday."

"Sorry buddy, I've been here for two years, no Jennifer here."

Our waitress left.

"That's odd. Jennifer served me my usual last night before I hit the casino and ran into you." I had still been reeling from our first meeting, the poetic beauty who refused to give me the time of day. I saw her through the windows of the Golden Gate Café, pouring coffee for patrons. I took a seat in the back of the Café. When she smiled and said, *Hello again,* I knew she had recognized me from my drunken haze in the Golden Nugget.

"As a matter of fact," I reached into the pocket of my jacket and pulled out a piece of paper that read: *Give me a call sometime, I'd like to gaze into those eyes over a glass of red wine—Jennifer—867-5309.* "I need to make a quick phone call, man. I'll be right back."

Of course, I had a nice shiny quarter in my pocket and the payphone was one of those blasted $1 phones. Wait, $1? When did that happen? I've seen 35 cents, even 45 cents in extreme cases, but never an entire dollar. Ludicrous. I pulled 75 additional cents from my pocket and gave it up; I needed to know what all the confusion was about. The number rang six times . . .

"Hello?" It was the voice of a man, desperately trying to hide the fact that he had run to the phone.

"Is Jennifer home?"

"Who the hell is this?" the man demanded.

"Who the hell is *this*?" I retaliated.

"I'm her husband . . . "

I couldn't speak.

"Is this Dean O'Leary?"

Wait, I didn't know Jennifer was married, and how the hell did this guy know my name?

"I can tell it's you. How dare you call this house, you bastard?"

"Now, hold on, mister. I don't know you, and besides knowing my name, I'm positive you don't know me."

"Oh, I know you; you're the scumbag that fucked my wife sixteen years ago and wrecked my family."

"You've got the wrong guy, pal, Jennifer gave me this number yesterday."

OK, now I was feeling like a person might right before they realize that they have lost their marbles for good.

"What? You got some sort of Rip Van Winkle complex? Look pal, the kids have moved out, Jennifer and I have been separated for years—that hooker is all yours. I hope it was worth it." He hung up.

This was turning out to be a *very* strange day.

"Did you find her?" Gaelin dutifully asked when I returned to the booth.

"No, wrong number." I didn't understand what had just taken place and figured hearing it second-hand would be that much more confusing. "Where the hell is our food?"

"I think they had to send someone to Wisconsin to get a fresh cow. I'm going to grab a paper. I'll be right back." Gaelin walked toward the front door.

What the hell was going on—who the hell was that guy on the phone—what the hell was his damage—where the hell was Jennifer—how the hell could we have slept together a decade ago—why the hell am I saying *hell* so much?

A shadow fell over my cup of coffee. Gaelin stood with white knuckles clutching the morning edition of the *Las Vegas Journal* as if it were his last faltering piece of reality. I've seen men with guns pressed to their temples, their eyes darting back and forth, waiting to die; I've seen men's faces as they opened their bedroom door to witness their loving wife straddling their best friend and whooping like a cowgirl on ecstasy—I have never seen terror like I saw in Gaelin's eyes.

"I'm positive that I don't want the answer to this question, but what's wrong Gaelin?"

He couldn't speak.

He dropped the paper in front of me and pointed to the upper right-hand corner.

July1, 2013

§

Gaelin and I had lost sixteen years in the blink of an eye, sprawled out on cold concrete, traveling through time in a catatonic state. We lost our consciousness and our wallets in 1997 and regained our consciousness in 2013. (Unfortunately, the wallets were still gone.)

"What does this mean?" Gaelin finally broke the silence.

"It means nothing. It means everything. It means that we live in 2013, I don't know." I was feigning calm, more for my benefit than Gaelin's.

"What are we going to do?"

"Well, I don't recall doing anything out of the ordinary that might trigger time travel, so I am assuming that this was not instigated. If that is the case, then we are probably stuck. If that's the case, we should make ourselves comfortable."

"How can you be so calm about this? We just lost sixteen years. We aren't the same people anymore. We're specters— the real Dean O'Leary is thirty-nine years old."

"If I survived to that age."

"Knock on wood, Dean. If you didn't believe in the supernatural before, you should now."

I rapped the table thrice with my knuckles. Once for Love and twice for Luck.

"I have money stashed all over the Caribbean. I should still be able to access it via passcode. Let's find a place to live and do what we can to come to grips with what's going on."

"OK, but I'm still having a problem dealing with the fact that we're walking around somewhere in this world on the verge of our forties."

I laughed out loud, "We should find ourselves, just for kicks."

"Hell, no. Didn't you see *Back To the Future*, Dean? Even accidentally seeing ourselves on the street could alter reality, as we know it. We may go back to a world ruled by puppy dogs." Gaelin smiled broadly.

"Rubbish. If anything altered, it would be 2013. I'd venture a guess that we are not existing in two planes of reality simultaneously. It's more likely you are a wild and particularly detailed hallucination. I've got a pretty strong feeling that this is our new home. This is the hand we've been dealt, let's play . . . to win."

Las Vegas was no longer a dense cluster of activity in the center of the valley. The City's tendrils reached to every cardinal point and pushed tensely against the surrounding hills and mountains. Vegas had burst and spread, infecting every sun-tortured inch of sand and devouring once-far-off mini-cities to the north and south. The economic boom had saturated the valley with cheap, brand-new homes. Development went wild until it all came crashing down in 2008. Gaelin and I took care of the shelter issue by finding a stranded ironworker from Kentucky who was willing to let his six-year-old home go for a song.

As soon as the deal was signed I went stir-crazy. On a particularly grey Thursday afternoon, instead of turning left onto Las Vegas Boulevard when leaving Caesar's, I swept down to Flamingo, hit 15 going south and never stopped.

I reached Hesperia at twilight.

The small silver rock marking Audene's resting place was gone. I knew the location by sight and knelt under the rapidly waning sun. I had hoped for this small sign of the familiar. *Hoped* may be a little understated. As the sun retreated behind the mountains to set on L.A., the long shadows began to blur the desert's stark lines. Nothing looked the same; nothing felt the same. I was free of Audene now. In this time, I was given another chance.

I sent a postcard to Gaelin from Victorville.

Gaelin,

On my way to Los Angeles by way of Hesperia.
Sorry for the abruptness of my departure.
I will be back.

As ever,
Dean

Los Angeles glimmered in the distance. Was I ready?

I followed a long train of revelers down Hollywood Boulevard. Someone had really done a number on the intersection of Hollywood and Vine. An immense, unseemly apartment complex attached to a vapid boutique hotel consumed the southeast block. Restaurants and bars you wouldn't expect to see until you crossed Highland had become the norm and the old crack-addict intersection was once again a bleeding altar to commerce.

The seedy one-night stand of a bar next to the Pantages Theatre had survived the neighborhood makeover; some things cannot be changed. The same mural graced the long wall of the Frolic Room, but now it was encased behind protective plastic sheeting. *Things must have gotten rough around here for a little while.* I didn't recognize anyone and it didn't look like anyone recognized me.

I ordered a Sapphire and tonic.

"Hey, when did all that mess across the street go up?"

The bartender rested against the back rail.

"Um, I'd say 2010 or so. But don't quote me on that," he smiled tiredly.

"Did they demolish the Taft Building?"

"The what?"

"The early last-century building on the corner where the hotel is."

"Oh, is that what it's called? Huh. Yeah, I think it's still there. Historical site, I think. Probably *can't* tear it down." — *That's exactly what I was counting on.*

The bartender flashed the same tired smile and walked the length of the bar looking for anyone in need of a refill. I paid my tab at last call and walked down Vine Street toward

Sunset. As long as the foundation of the Taft Building remained intact, I had an emergency source of funds buried beneath the legendary intersection.

"Who is this?" Perturbed.

"Gaelin?" Slurring.

"Dean? Fuck, man, you OK?" Concerned.

"Fine, fine, why not? I had, I mean I *think* I had too much to drink. Gaelin, I had too much to drink." Dismissive.

"Huh. That's a serious statement. Where are you?" Absent.

"I don't know. I just don't know. I am, I mean I am somewhere. Somewhere, OK? I'm working on it, I'm working. Working. Working." Confused.

"Dean, are you still there? Dean? Good. Are you in Vegas? No?" Gaelin had to hide his laughter as his friend tried to swim through a sea of ethyl to form a sentence. "Sounds like L.A. Do you need me to call someone for you, can you make it back to wherever you're staying?" Compassionate.

"No, no. I'm sorry. I don't know why I called. Gaelin?"

"Yes?"

"I'll be back."

"I believe you, man."

"Good. Night. Good . . . "

I began writing. On napkins, on second-rate motel stationary, on post-its: whatever came to mind. Soon, I had compiled an impressive stack of hand-written scraps of pages. These missives were sodden by scattered thoughts, inner monologues and bits of journal-like reportage. It wasn't much, but I was finally writing. I drove back into the Vegas Valley several weeks later.

"Welcome back." Gaelin greeted me calmly.

"Thanks. Sorry about the..."

"Enough said." He smiled.

Life became what it had to: Neither of us were tethered to 2013, we owed the world around us nothing, and the world offered nothing in return. I had come to expect little from the world, and time is only an indication of decay; each day was like the next, neither worse nor better—stasis. No time period is universally worse than another. All of the difference lies in who's written the history book. The downtrodden will paint a painful picture, and the victorious will sing the century's praises.

Gaelin got a job to break up the days and nights while I retreated into silence and gave a half-hearted try at writing again. Gaelin hoped to find friends, or at least modern distractions, but like my pointless typing, neither of us were granted external peace or acceptance. He eventually quit his job and joined me in pissing away day after day. Gaelin and I became inseparable because we had no one else.

"Wake up asshole, get dressed. It's time to celebrate." Gaelin struck me repeatedly.

"Whuh? Whuh's going on?" Waking up is traumatic. "What are we celebrating?"

"Your birthday, idiot. Get the hell up, it's almost midnight."

"OK, OK, I'm up. How old am I?" I sincerely wanted to know . . .

"Two martinis, please. Top shelf," Gaelin addressed the heavily pierced, semi-clad bartender—the Double Down was not known for being a classy place. A decade's worth of collected filth and graffiti consumed every wall from floor to ceiling. The Double Down was a pungent bouquet of bodily fluids and gallons of beer that had penetrated the concrete floors and come to rest, forming a foul layer of sediment.

"Well, you're a quarter of a century old Dean, living in the not-so-distant future with a guy you knew previously for about six hours. Bet you didn't fathom life could take a twist like this." Gaelin raised his highball glass and clinked it against mine.

"Could anyone?" I sarcastically retorted.

"Honestly, Dean, do you ever hope we'll make it back?"

An interesting and valid question indeed.

"Back to what? I was staring down the barrel of a short bout of serious personal destruction and a hopefully painless exeunt. No one even knows I'm a criminal in this time, so no . . . do you?"

"I don't know, part of me does. If, for nothing else, just to feel like a part of the Human Race again. We exist outside of reality now; I do miss the mortal coil." Gaelin stared at the mirror behind the bar. We were trapped men; the bars of our cage were beyond our view.

"We exist outside of the mortal coil now—make your peace with that. We didn't ask for this and we have no choice but to play it out."

Gaelin sat silently. He hadn't successfully detached from 1997 yet. It didn't take me long after returning from L.A. I chose to look at it as someone would look at moving to a nicer neighborhood: You're still you, people are still imbeciles, and the rich still run things. The only difference is that you pay way too much money for rent, on a different patch of dirt than before. Something still plagued my mind: I needed to know what happened to Dean O'Leary. In the event that we accidentally stumbled back into 1997, I'd like to know how to prevent any misfortune that should have befallen me.

"Gaelin?"

"Yes?"

"This place sucks."

"Buck up, birthday boy, the night is young."

The barkeep walked over, handed me a Newcastle, and said, "You single?"

"Who's asking?" The bartender was definitely not my type.

"Answer the question, smart guy."

"Yes, very."

"In that case, this is for you, regards of the young lady at the table."

I didn't even turn to see who she was.

"Tell her: thank you very much, this is a first for me, and I am flattered beyond words."

"Sure pal, whatever." The bartender walked back across the empty bar and relayed the message. She smiled and I averted my stare.

That was true: No stranger had ever purchased a beer for me and sent it through the bartender. It was coy and flirtatious. My experience with women thus far could be better described as aggressive and cold.

"Aren't you going to go talk to her?" Gaelin prodded.

"No, I'm not good at barroom wit. Besides, she's sitting with someone."

"Don't be an asshole, Dean. The woman's not going to send you a drink and ask if you're single if that's her man."

"Shut up, I'm justifying my fear. Drink up, let's get out of here."

"At least look at her."

The last thing I needed was . . .

"No, thanks. Finish your beer and let's get out of this pit."

"OK, you big baby, let's go. We've got more drinking to do." Gaelin sank the rest of his beer and walked toward the toilet.

The woman was stunning. Her icy eyes could compel completely for centuries. She wore a crisp emerald dress whose lines evoked thoughts of a young Evelyn Ankers. All I wanted was to be moved by someone and to feel that I moved them in return. Nothing unique there.

By looking over my shoulder at this woman, I had been stricken by a familiar fear. Until now, I have been quite comfortable with the idea that I would grow old alone. But the reality of how alone we . . . I . . . truly was had me questioning the wisdom of solitude. The way our eyes met, I knew I could give it all to her and thank her for crushing my heart. I gluttonously continued to glance over my shoulder and *accidentally* make eye contact. I could lose myself to this woman and that scared me. However, it nauseated me to think I may never see her again.

Her severely cut pin-up bangs lent a note of seriousness to her otherwise long, playful, auburn hair. She deftly collected her tresses and pinned them back—revealing her opulent, porcelain neck—as I casually watched. I rose and made my way over to this mysterious woman. I reached for her hand and I felt myself let go of control and try again. I was consumed; there was no hope for me.

"Thank you, I am flattered beyond words."

"That's what I heard. I'm Selene."

That voice could say the simplest words and I would remain rapt.

"I'm Dean."

"Ah, yes, of course you are." She and her companion laughed quietly. He rose and bade us farewell with a sly smile.

I was confused: "What did I miss?"

"We were trying to decide who you looked like. I had you pegged as a substantially more attractive William Burroughs in his twenties. Oso, my friend, said you looked more like the fragile Kerouac type."

"But my name is Dean." I smiled.

"Which means you are neither. You are the self-styled Casanova and adventurer that eluded Kerouac and struck Burroughs as a maniac."

She was becoming frightfully perfect by the sentence, so I played along, "Which is quite an admonishment coming from the Gentleman Junky."

She smiled brightly; we'd plucked one another's intellectual strings and our concerto was beginning to crescendo.

"Be careful, Dean—I'll show you why Anaïs was never far from Henry's mind."

"Be careful, yourself; this time, there's no June to stand between us."

Gaelin exited the bathroom.

"I must leave. Will I see you again?"

"You will, Mr. Miller, you will."

I whispered, "My sweet, delicate, Anaïs." She smiled sensuously as I touched my lips to her hand. When I pulled my hand from hers, the pain was undeniable. After all this, had I found *Her* here? In this bar, in this time? Elation tinted by doubt clouded my smile. I turned so that she wouldn't see.

§

"Good morning, sunshine."

"Fuck you, Gaelin. Why are you waking me up?"

"Because I need to give you your presents." What could I say? I wanted to sleep so badly, but the man wanted to shower me with gifts, and he was as giddy as a Catholic schoolgirl at a Boy Scout convention.

"All right, all right, I'm up." I walked into the living room.

"Bad news: I didn't get you anything. That was a lie. I have something potentially world- and Earth-shattering to tell you, but first, the good news: you lost consciousness around 3:00 a.m., and you kept muttering Anaïs, Anaïs, I love you, I NEED YOU." Gaelin barely suppressed laughter.

"Don't mock me."

"I drove back to the Double Down and spoke to the young lady who purchased your Newcastle. She came by this morning and left this but refused to stay." Gaelin handed me a brown parchment envelope. My heart leapt with excitement. I opened the envelope.

"Anaïs . . . Selene," I corrected myself.

"Can't say. She wouldn't tell me, and she wouldn't give me her number either."

"Why not?"

"She said that the two of you were destined for each other and that she knew you would find her if it took centuries. Sounds like she's playing games."

My fingers found a piece of paper deep inside the envelope.

Dearest Mr. H. Miller,

I am caught in the immense jaws of your desire,
I feel myself dissolving, ripping open to your descent.
I feel myself yielding to your dark hunger, my feelings
Smoldering, rising from me like smoke from a black mass.
Take me; take my gifts and my words, and my body
And my cries and my joys and my terror and my abandon.
Take all that you desire.

Take me as if I were something you want to possess,
Inside your body like a fuel. Take me as if I were a food
Needed for daily sustenance. I throw everything into the
Jaws of your desire and hunger. I throw all I have known,
Experienced, and given before now.

Love,
Anaïs

"She is playing a game, Gaelin, and I'm all in." How could she be any more perfect? She moved me on so many levels. Her beauty enamored me, I adored her sense of style,

I was thrust into ecstatic pleasure by her mystery, and I was in awe of her mind. I was hers.

"I must find her." I rushed past Gaelin. I called over my shoulder as I descended the stairs, "You're a good man, Gaelin Gilbraunsen, no matter what your mom says." I showered and shaved with the ferocity of a hurricane and threw on my best suit.

"I'm going to find her."

"Woah. Just like that? You don't even know where this person lives, Dean."

"Doesn't matter. I'll find her."

"Look man, no offense," Gaelin lit a cigarette, "it just seems like you fall head over heels for every girl that turns your head.

"I don't take offense to that. Anything else?"

"I guess not."

I wandered Las Vegas Boulevard for hours, on a hunch. Searching for Selene. Praying for a glimpse. A glimpse of my perceived perfection. Knowing full well that I could not be satisfied until I possessed this woman completely, as she now possessed me. The sun began setting, but my intensity did not wane. Then, out of the corner of my eye, I saw silken ivory legs crossed sensuously under a magnificent, knee-length, navy skirt. She was staring directly at me over a steaming cup of tea. I rushed to her side, wrapped my arms around her waist and lifted her out of her chair. She dropped her cup and our lips embraced to the sound of delicate smashing porcelain. The very molecules of the universe stood still and silent in reverence for our lovers' embrace. I was right: This union was perfect, I had no doubts, and I had no questions that were unanswered. Her lips were sweeter

William M. Brandon III

than the lover's wine Cleopatra shared with Antony, more permanent than the poison Juliet drew from Romeo's lips, and more perfect than a full moon's light cast on a dark sea. Our lips parted, I whispered in her ear, "I never want to be apart from you—be with me until the end."

"Yes, yes, a thousand times, yes."

We lost all sense of the world around us. I pulled her into a side corridor of the café and began to cover her body with the caress of my lips and my pleading hands. I pressed her against the wall and dove into her flesh, needing to be deeper, to be closer, to be inside her, to be a part of her. She whined and wrapped a long, sensuous leg around my waist as her hand began unbuttoning my trousers. She moaned when she felt my desire for her. She guided me toward her, between her thighs, and clasped her hands around my hips as I plunged deep into her silken flesh. She swayed rhythmically against me and wrapped her arms around my neck. I placed my hands firmly on my obsession's smooth, enticing hips and thrust deeper and deeper. I felt her clenching, never wanting to let me withdraw. I felt her fingernails digging passionately into my neck as she begged me not to stop. Her body quivered as she released her grip. I leaned my head back and felt my body shake as a sensual tidal wave rushed through my body. We were barely able to breathe as we held each other against gravity's forces.

"Get out of here before I alert the police . . . perverts." The world came sharply into focus. We giggled like children. I buttoned my trousers and darted with my love on my arm out into the cool evening air. All was perfect, all was right . . .

Schizophrenia

Days of passion and reckless abandon. Give myself completely or lose my Love forever? Lose my Love completely or give myself forever? Hours of contemplation on her eyes and none on myself. Hours of pining for her scent, for her flesh against mine, inside of me, around me, occupying my whole person. It's maddening that she holds this power over me. I'm the one who has all the answers, the one who never skips a beat, the one who has learned to never sell himself out.

She has reached her love into my throat and gripped my very being, ripped it from this broken vessel and surrounded it with warmth, emotion, happiness, and, most of all, Love. The most pressing question is *why?*

She deserves a man who sees only beauty in this vile world. A man who cannot fathom the pain of faithlessness. A man who has not felt the intricacies of betrayal or its aftermath. She deserves this, yet I can't see past my own fear and let go. I don't deserve her, and one day she will realize this. I will be left with my heart in my hand. Can I keep my tortured head above water long enough to show her how much I love her, or will I drown before we can look each other in the eye?

Questions. Questions. Questions. You can ask me questions for the rest of your life and you'll never find what you're looking for until you look into my eyes. I've felt every pain, every joy, every disappointment, every betrayal. I've heard every spiteful word that could ever pass your lips. I've heard it again and again, and my resilience is gone. It's completely gone. I don't bounce back like I used to. I want to be alone. I want no eyes on me. I want everyone in this world to forget that I exist. Stop judging me, stop questioning me, I'm above that, and so are you. It all fades, it all leaves. People leave, love leaves, health runs, joy is gone. The simple things are gone. They have come, ripped my heart out, and walked away. Very slowly with feet that move at the pace of years per step, dragging the ground, making the horrible sound of EXIT.

The sound of the stream is deafening. Who says you can't hear erosion? Your warmth has eroded the ice and stone I've so carefully built around my love. You claw at my defenses to reach inside, to feel connected, truly connected with me. You're saving me. I see forever in your eyes, and for once, I'm not afraid. It breathes fire into my veins. It inspires me. You inspire me to no end. I needed you last night. I needed to feel you, to touch your porcelain skin. I needed to caress the flesh that so binds me to this earth, the flesh that addicted me, that trapped me in your arms. I'm helpless. I hope one day I'll have the strength to show you that. To whisk you away where nobody can hurt us anymore. Where we can simply be in love without outside intervention. I want evenings that don't end despite the inevitable sunrise. I want to conquer your heart, and submit my heart and my will to you.

He is a good man, who has a hard time showing it. Caught up in the *nothing can hurt me because I've already been destroyed* mentality. Supernova waiting to happen—a bright shining star—in a hurry to burn out.

I'm more in love than I have ever thought possible. She consumes me. Positively consumes me. An improper blink of an eye or furrow of the brow, or pulling away of her lips from mine sends me into convulsions of paranoia. Instantaneous fear that her love will someday wane.

Segue to destruction—the end of a century, the beginning of the end—the beginning of the Little One's century, only four years' time and torn asunder—the little one of the twenty-first century—dear Sator, alive and dead in the twentieth—can the twenty-first be any different?—and the twenty-fourth day of March, he enters his twenty-third— eighty years over twenty-three years—intertwined.

I've lived my life and now I only exist. Observing painfully, Life around and throughout. It's a free feeling of disassociation. But I have connected with two. One, my eternal lover and one, a love I will never acknowledge. Today has been lovely, absolutely lovely. My pen chases page after page and my inspiration is seemingly infinite. This is what happens when you ascend and look at the world from distant stars—DETACHMENT—such negative connotations to such perfection. Detach and be free, choose to adhere and lose your chance to choose. Draw close to the human race, and the ignorant masses will destroy your Life with obsessions.

Consume—Consume—Destroy—
Must Create—Must Earn—Must Give—Fuck—Sleep—
Live—Communicate
The worst of these: communication.

Disengage now . . . for your own sake.

DAMNED NONSENSE. Rubbish. I'm so violently ill and disturbed by all the fucking nonsense. The last pages of the book meant to save your literary soul are nonsense. No intelligent, cohesive thought, nothing to gain, all is lost, time, love, interest, money. I'm frustrated. I feel an abysmal emptiness as I turn the last page, as my eyes peruse the last words. Give me something, please, I beg of you, give me something to cling to, something to identify with, allow me to identify with you. It never happens. Why can't I identify with something tangible? Most of the people I truly identify with are below the ground. No chance for verbal discourse, no chance for examination of thoughts; interpretation is all one-sided—dead end. I met a person once who spoke my language. I felt so close; I felt a strange shyness when we spoke, when our gazes met. We knew each other's thoughts and we were unified on a mental plane that cannot be reached by most humans. Now, we are as distant with each other as we are with the majority of the human race. The connection has faded, and I will regret it forever.

—Nonsense. Rubbish—

Can I feel a connection when I am so defended? Why desire a connection at all? What weakness exists in my mind that begs for someone to say *Yes, I understand—yes, I love you—the real you—I won't ask anything of you-you are my perfection—I need you.* This has never happened, it probably never will; all expect alteration to fulfill their needs.

—Misery loves company. I know she feels the same—

Dean O'Leary
Las Vegas
2013

The Necessity of Adversity II

We were married the next day before the honorable Judge Andrea Deamos. She smiled and gave us her personal blessing based on the testimony. We glowed. People's face's twisted in jealousy and disgust when they saw how repulsively smitten we were with each other. We spent our days roaming the city drinking fine wine, dining in exquisite restaurants, and making love in public places. It only took one sultry innuendo and we would be caught in our tangled web—misplaced (purposely) hands, and the precious marriage of lips against flesh. Once the game began, we were at war with our environment, the very environment keeping us clothed and polite. Yet, her hand on my wool slacks or my hand slipping slowly to the small of her back as we discussed *The Second Sex* would inevitably result in a thorough check of exits and staff. When the coast was clear, we would repair to a darkened corridor or a locked lavatory, returning with the blissful glistening of lovers' guilt painted playfully on our faces.

We spent our evenings in each other's arms by candlelight, gazing into each other's eyes and speaking about everything that crossed our minds. We stopped briefly only to smoke cigarettes between intense lovemaking and uninspired searches for sustenance yet never seemed to quench our thirsts for each other's flesh. We were all any human could ask for from love and much more. I never thought it possible for two individuals to be such a perfect union, to be one person. Our nights lasted beyond the rising sun and we did not sleep for fear we may be wasting our last precious moments together.

"Dean!"

"What is it, my love?" I was surprised by her sudden calling out.

"What's missing from this picture?"

Selene lay naked before me; nothing was missing, and nothing more was necessary. She held her hand up to me, asking me to stay focused.

"What's missing?"

"Your wedding ring. We forgot rings."

"Yes," she smiled shyly.

After a long discussion about the horrors faced by third-world miners of precious stones and metals, we decided on stainless-steel bands. Perfect, beautiful, and slavery-free.

"Now it's official Mrs. O'Leary, you belong to me in the traditional sense." I smiled, a proud groom.

"I belong to myself—you're just officially the first and last person I want to see every day for the rest of my life."

"Touché gorgeous, touché." I kissed her deeply on the corner of Maryland Parkway and Tropicana before hailing a cab.

We did our best to keep polite company over the course of the next few weeks. Selene's friends were very warm and accepting, but neither Selene nor I truly desired to waste our time surrounded by other people. Our distracted attention was focused on us two, and all else — conversation, company, and setting — melted into the background of our framed portrait of perfection.

Private engagements were much worse. We were a bore to all concerned, and given the opportunity, we would slip out of sight, into a garden, into a master suite, into a deserted kitchen, and set about exploring one another's clothed bodies until we were discovered or the weight of our absence became too great to explain away with cigarette breaks or phone calls. Soon, we were no longer accepted in polite company and the short-lived invitations ceased.

The happiness I had promised myself had finally overwhelmed me and I left my doubts behind.

"Damn."

"What's the matter dearest?" My still-blushing bride inquired breathily.

"I should call Gaelin and let him know I'm alive."

I hadn't spoken to Gaelin since my birthday . . . over a month ago.

"Hello?"

"Gaelin, it's Dean."

"Dean. I thought you were dead for certain."

"I am. Dead to the world I knew before, and reborn into the arms of Love."

"Wow, that's an intense statement, even for you. Are you leaving Las Vegas?"

"No, not that I know of, why?"

"Just curious. I would love to take the two of you to dinner so that I can meet this mysterious woman whose charms have wooed this century's best candidate for bitter, lonely, old man. Ms. Nin is it?" he asked in jest.

"Mrs. O'Leary."

"You're married? Congratulations, Dean. It's settled: We're having dinner tonight. Be here at 9:00 p.m., I'll take care of the rest."

"We graciously accept."

"Fabulous, then I'll see you tonight." He hung up.

I couldn't explain to Gaelin how important it was to me that he was so happy for Selene and I. He could have been bitter toward my love, but once again, he had shown that he was a true friend.

We met Gaelin at the house. He greeted Selene like a dear old friend and I could tell she wooed him as soon as she spoke. Her elocution was mesmerizing.

"Let's get going, I'll drive," Gaelin insisted. "I have a surprise for you, Dean."

We drove up Sahara and stopped in front of an enormous supermarket. "We're here."

"We're eating at a supermarket?" I wanted to know.

"I don't think Gaelin would take us to a supermarket for dinner," Selene defended Gaelin.

"Thank you, Selene," Gaelin kissed her delicate hand. "I barely know you and already I swear that if Dean betrays you, I shall take care of you without blinking an eye."

"Easy there, Casanova," I struck back.

We walked through the grocery store to the meat cutter's stand and Gaelin muttered something in Spanish to the attendant. The attendant motioned for a young man to his left to cover the counter for him and asked that we follow him. We walked through a series of locked doors and staircases.

We emerged into a large, dimly lit, smoky room.

"I can't believe it."

"What is it darling?" my lovely wife asked.

"This is the restaurant where Gaelin and I first crossed paths. I thought it was torn down in the mid-2000s."

"The government tore it down. The proprietors were indicted for giving aid and support to a terrorist organization. Namely, the Castro government. The owners' only son went underground and recreated his parents' pride and joy within the walls of this supermarket with the help of fellow Cuban ex-pats also keeping a low profile. The owners still languish in holding cells, ironically, on the very Caribbean island they sought to defend."

"Heartbreaking and incredible." I held my hat over my heart out of respect.

"Booth 13 please, Romario." Gaelin smiled as he said this and gestured to the man who had escorted us through the supermarket. We sat directly under the masterpiece that had served as introduction for Gaelin and I—our unspoken appreciation for the painting comprised our first mutual memory. I felt at home. The love of my life and my only friend, together here and now . . . I was waiting to push pause on the recording of Time and feel this perfection forevermore.

Gaelin fell in love with Selene immediately. He couldn't get enough of her ideas on the Dadaist pamphlets and El Greco, and after casual greetings, he had ignored me completely. They talked and talked, and it brought an enormous smile to my face. After we had finished desert, we had drinks. The whiskey was undeniably perfect. My love excused herself from the table and Gaelin anxiously reached for the pocket of his jacket and removed a folded piece of newspaper.

"I couldn't bear it after you disappeared, I had to find out what was supposed to happen to us."

"What do you mean?"

"While you were in Los Angeles, I took advantage of the quite modern facilities at UNLV and researched our names. Not surprisingly, I didn't turn up, but I did find a few news articles about *Dean O'Leary*."

"Great," I added sarcastically. "What the hell did I do? What bit of nastiness would I have become?"

"Be certain you want to know, Dean. If you are, I'll gladly tell you, but if you are not sure . . . you're happy now, so it almost doesn't matter."

"That's completely unfair. Now you've piqued my interest, and I need to know."

He handed me the newspaper article.

"You died in 1998. According to this article, three unidentified suspects and a man identified as Dean O'Leary robbed a Las Vegas bank in 1998. *They identified the body as Dean O'Leary*, wanted for robbing banks all over California. You were shot through the neck during a high-speed pursuit. The other three got away and were never identified."

"I don't know how to feel about this." Untrue. I felt my mind slipping from me and my concentration receding. I was dead. Shot through the neck. I looked down at my hands; I gripped my empty glass to feel its density. I was still here. I had to be. "Whatever brought us here prolonged my life. I thought this was a curse. Now I can't deny that it was necessary. I met the love of my life, I could never bear missing out on that." *Odd, that means I would have died when*

Selene was nine years old. It was probably better that I had died; I was doomed die alone, as I had always feared.

"Here she comes, Dean. Unless you think now is the time to discuss where you came from, I'd put that away." I slid the paper into my coat pocket. I wasn't sure if this was something Selene should ever know. It was her right to know, but a better time would surely present itself. "Hello, my lover. Shall we blow this joint and paint this dreary town red?"

"Yes, my love," Selene purred.

"Ready, middle-aged man?" Gaelin jibed.

"Let's swing," I answered.

We made our way from casino to casino, quickly making disgusting amounts of money and spending it just as rapidly. The world seemed to be on its knees begging to give all the pleasures it had to offer to the three of us.

"Caesar's Palace?" Gaelin offered carefully.

"Yes, let's go," I drunkenly agreed.

We had stayed away from Caesar's Palace. It was no secret that the place gave us both the creeps after what had happened. Time to stop living in the past, time to start living now.

We strode into Caesar's like two kings and a queen. We couldn't lose to save our lives, and before we knew it, we had received everything but complimentary heroin from the hotel staff. We were all positioned around a dealer who seemed to be making a fool out of my darling and I, but losing his shirt to Gaelin. Selene and I stopped playing and just watched the dealer and Gaelin face off poker hand after poker hand. The more I watched this dealer—the way he arrogantly tapped the rail while he waited for players to make a move—the more I felt I knew him from somewhere. I caught Gaelin's gaze and we both simultaneously realized that this was the dealer we had faced on that fateful evening in 1997.

"How long have you worked here . . . Ryan?" He looked surprised that I knew his name, but quickly remembered that he was wearing a name badge.

"Oh, about eighteen years, give or take." Even his sincere smile contained a challenge: *Feeling lucky? I dare you.*

"Ever face as worthy an adversary?" I asked, gesturing to Gaelin as he brushed his hair away from his glasses. Gaelin was just nerdy enough to be considered a non-threat and he played it up whenever he could.

"No," the dealer answered, "but I always win in the end."

This was definitely the same guy. His cockiness hadn't waned in seventeen years. A young woman arrived with our three glasses of wine, and after tipping her heavily and receiving that *come hither* stare, Gaelin raised his glass, "I propose a toast. To my best friend and his eternal love . . . if she can stand him that long . . . may a lifetime of memories be made and may you both be kept safely wrapped in each other's arms."

"Here, here. To kinky sex and longevity," I retorted.

"Dealer, $1,000 on this next hand. You're about to lose again, and then we must bid thee farewell for greener pastures." The dealer scowled like a bitter old man and slid the cards to Gaelin slowly.

The dealer looked like he had seen a ghost. He recognized Gaelin.

I looked at Gaelin. His eyes were wide open with terror; his white knuckles clutched his cards as if they were his last faltering piece of reality. I had only seen Gaelin like this on one other occasion. Gaelin couldn't speak; his face was twisted with pain, misery, and intense thought.

After a long silence, Gaelin laid his cards down. "Number of the Beast over kings."

As soon as the words rolled off Gaelin's lips the dealer laid his cards down.

"Dealer has three aces." Ryan smiled stoically. He had never had any doubt about the outcome.

The light around the dealer began to distort and bend. I looked to my love.

"Dean . . . " she whispered, unable to breathe. I reached for her and clasped my arms around her shoulders. I felt the invisible hands of Time wrap around my body over and over like cloth around a corpse.

"I love you, I will love you for all time . . . " Our lips met. I knew I would never see her again. I was pulled from her grasp and the world went black.

§

I faced myself. I looked directly into my own eyes.

"Hello, Dean," this person said.

"Where am I?" I asked.

This person was now the dealer.

"An interesting question, more importantly, are you comfortable?"

"Is this hell?"

"No, heaven and hell don't exist. And now, neither do you. You have departed from the world of the living and come to me. You are in a dimension of introspect. Continuous, stringent, self examination."

"Sounds like hell to me."

"It can be if you so desire," my host was now Gaelin. "Or this can be eternal rejuvenation and understanding. Humans run about like ants under a magnifying glass their entire lives asking a single, question: WHY? We can discover the answers together."

"Why have you ripped me away from my eternal love?"

This person's interpretation of Audene whispered, "That was not my doing, Dean. I simply sweep up the mess, I don't instigate change."

"I don't want knowledge—I want life." I looked away from Audene. It was a cruel tactic.

"Then, I will leave you to your hell." Selene turned on her heel and began to walk away.

"Wait. Please, don't leave me alone, now," I begged in dire, desperate frustration. "I almost had everything . . . " I muttered quietly, defeated.

"You have a lesson to learn, old man." I faced myself again, age eleven. "Adversity makes you think. Without it, decisions don't exist. Without decisions, there are no options. Without options, there is no reason to think." Age sixteen . . . "If you do not face adversity, your path is clear and so is your mind. Ever wonder why overtly religious people have that glazed-over look in their eyes? No options."

I started laughing. Odd that I'd get humor from an archetype as serious as Death.

"Enjoy the beauty of adversity; let it flow through and around you. Push against it and you will find direction." Age twenty-five . . . "Let it push against you and be swept away in aimless frustration."

Death was suddenly distracted.

"Goodbye, Dean."

Goodbye? What did he mean? I started coughing. Bright, white light began flooding into my eyes, awakening my senses. People rushed about above me.

White uniforms, latex gloves, silver badges . . .

Blood from my chest poured through the latex-clad fingers of a young EMT.

Darkness.

"He's back, we've got him. I thought we'd lost him."

I thrashed against the gurney.

"Calm down, you've been shot. We're taking you to an operating room."

The mask on my face began dispensing its invitation from Morpheus.

"Gaelin!" I bellowed, hoping it rose to a *shout*.

"Your friend is fine. Please, just relax and breathe deeply."

"How do you feel?"

"Like shit." Every grimace-inducing movement took total effort. "What happened?"

"You were involved in a shooting—I'd stop moving around so much, helps with the pain—and you've been unconscious for nine days. The bullet entered your back, hit your left ninth rib and barely missed piercing your lung."

"I don't remember . . . "

"He shot you in the back, Mr. O'Leary, probably while you laid there unconscious. Get comfortable—you're not going anywhere anytime soon." The doctor turned to leave.

"Where's Gaelin?" I called out.

"Your friend was released. He should be here anytime. He comes every day."

I woke as Gaelin entered the room.

"Dean, they told me you were awake. How are you?"

"Good, I guess. Didn't die. Still don't feel exactly *rooted*. Do you?"

"More like *up*rooted . . . "

"Good. I don't know what to think about what happened. How am I supposed to . . . "

"Look Dean, you're going to heal up and be back at the tables in no time. Don't let a couple of thugs ruin your life."

"Thugs? I wasn't talking about thugs. I was talking about Selene . . . "

" . . . what happened to us happens to people all over the world every hour of every day. Who is Selene?"

"Se—" Had I gone mad? "When you say *what happened to us*, what are you referring to?"

"Getting knocked in the head—in your case, shot, as well—and being robbed. Did you lose your memory, too, man?" Gaelin laughed uncomfortably.

He didn't remember. Or, more frighteningly, I had lost my mind.

Gaelin and I parted ways once he felt assured that I was on the road to recovery. With no shared memory of what had happened to us, we were strangers and our inaugural experience as friends had been violent and unpleasant by any person's standards. I couldn't let go of my images of Selene. I refused to believe that it was all an elaborate hallucination. Whether Gaelin remembered or not, he receded into the neon blur and I retreated to North Las Vegas to erase Selene from my mind.

Confrontation

White, wispy smoke wound itself between and around the long strands of midday light that bisected my room. I followed the pillar of smoke to its source, cradled between two fingers. Two fingers on a hand adorned only by a single shining steel band. My mornings began the same. Before I could inhale my first deep breathe of oxygen, I fumbled for my cigarettes, and with a flick of my thumb and a strike of flint, I was inhaling the perfect ivory smoke that curled and spiraled in the sunlight that pierced through my window. This smoke, as transparent and light as it appeared, obscured the sunlight.

I could never again have her . . . my true love. She was the only beacon of light I had found in this cruel, destructive world. Since losing my darling Selene, I left the house for two reasons and two reasons only: alcohol and cigarettes. Nothing else mattered to me. Without alcohol, I had no motivation, no drive, no need to better myself or even try. I needed it to function—I had sunk beneath the surface.

I transplanted myself to a small studio apartment on the north side of Las Vegas. The rent and conditions were meager, but I was in no mood to wallow in luxury. I simply needed to achieve a constant state of inebriation, fuck all else. Gunshots rang out all around, day and night, and somehow, I found this comforting. I had even decided to join in on the decadence and found great pleasure shooting at the wall in my studio as I lay in bed, smoking and drinking the hours away. After three months (and three times as many visits from the police and assorted authorities), my wall became a great crater-ridden monument to my angst. I was careful not to shoot out my window, but I had shot through the wall on two occasions. It had occurred to me at the time to fear that my bullet had found a target outside of my tiny universe, but that involved caring about something other than myself, and that no longer appealed to me.

Under my solitary window was a wooden desk with a 1940 Underwood typewriter resting snugly on its surface. Next to my typewriter was a tall, sensuous flask of whiskey. It was time for breakfast. I stumbled to my desk, barely opening my eyes to the afternoon sun. I stared at the Underwood as I poured a belt. Who was I kidding? I had never been a writer. Suffering was supposed to feed a writer's creativity, yet I could barely lift a finger to press a key.

I used my index finger, between drags off my cigarette, to type:

d-e-p-r-e-s-s-i-o-n.

That was actually progress. What can I say? I looked out the window at the wind whipping through the streets. The children didn't play in the street in this neighborhood; they made business transactions on the corners, rolled dice against the steps of my building, and occasionally walked straight up to each other, drew their guns, and murdered their playmates on the cold, grey pavement. I turned around; my apartment was tiny, dreary. The grey walls of the single room were broken twice, once by a dark closet door, once by the black front door. Light was a luxury; one I rather liked denying myself. I retreated to the warmth of my bed with my breakfast. I rolled over and picked up a copy of *On the Road*. I promised myself that I would read it once a month in hopes that its powers would provoke me to get up and go, to do something . . . it always had before. I lit another cigarette. Only three left. I'd have to get up and go out soon. After three pages, Kerouac's subtle optimism began to seem sad and naive. I set the book down and stared at the holes in the wall. Why me? Why couldn't I have gone through life not knowing Selene? This sense of loss was too much for me to bear; this depression had taken over, consumed me from within, and slowly, very slowly, eaten away at my very core. A tidal wave of emotion rampaged through my head and, as rapidly, receded. One cigarette left; time to get up.

I wiped away a circle in the condensation on the bathroom mirror. In a third-person daze, I ran my hands over months' worth of beard. I looked like a completely different person. I slicked my hair back as I always had—it was an odd combination of disorder and control.

I wanted Selene. I wanted what was; I wanted the future. If I couldn't have it, I preferred to rot away . . . slowly.

I stepped out into the late afternoon sun. It was one of those rare days in Vegas when the sun was mostly obscured by the clouds. The clouds above me had seen fit to clear a sunlit path to the liquor store . . . kismet. I pulled the collar of my jacket up around my neck, tucked my hands into the pockets, and began the block-long jaunt to Andy's Liquor-Beer-&-Wine-Emporium (carefully following the path carved by our father Sol).

Electronic doors opened to the stylings of the *Stayin' Alive* soundtrack. Andy "D" was the owner of this fine alcohol-dispensing establishment and a movie addict in denial. Andy knew every line, every scene, and every actor or actress from every movie you or anyone else on this spinning globe had ever seen. One sentence of dialogue could evoke title, character, and situation instantaneously. Andy was a perplexing fellow. He was raised in a wealthy family and bided his time with them until he completed his degree as a sound engineer. Straight out of school, Andy happened upon a quirky band from Southern California that piqued his interest and took them under his aural wing. Andy sunk five years and a great deal of money into this band, recording and mixing their music for pennies. Then it happened . . . they hit the BIG TIME. Platinum record after platinum record made Andy "D" a very wealthy man. Musicians from all over the world paid incredible amounts of money for Andrew to merely oversee their recording sessions. With this newfound wealth, Andy purchased several business chains that he ran from afar in between recording sessions. He always had a smile on his face, mostly for P.R. reasons, and never showed negativity on the outside. He was in Vegas for six weeks on vacation, and I enjoyed seeing him more often.

"Dean, how they hangin'?"

"To the left. Why the hell are you still here? You know I can't steal when you're around. Shouldn't you be in

California crammed into a mixing room with five rockstars and their bimbo girl-toys?"

"Dean, Dean, Dean, always trying to get rid of me."

"Actually, it's good to see you. What's new in the *high alcohol content* section?"

"I have some serious vino from the Motherland arriving this evening, definitely worth checking out. A little expensive, but since it's you . . . "

"*Higher* content. Andy, my boy, I only drown my sorrows in whiskey."

"Well, I'm sure you know where to find everything. Help yourself. Oh yeah, Dean, we also received a shipment of Bombay Sapphire today." Gin. It had been a while since gin passed my lips. That thought reminded me of the good old days . . . damn, I sounded old.

"Thank you, kind sir. I shall return."

Let's see, six-pack of Guinness, six-pack of Newcastle, Chivas, Bombay Sapphire gin . . . what the hell? It'd been too long.

"Drew, ring this up and make it snappy, the alcohol's a calling me."

"What are you doing to . . . I mean *with* yourself these days? Are you gainfully employed?"

"Let's just say I'm *independently wealthy*."

"Why the hell do you live in this part of town?"

"It's a long, sordid tale Drew, and I have drinking to do."

"I'm sorry, Dean. I didn't mean to offend you."

"None taken. It's just been an interesting couple of years for me, and I'm a little touchy as a result."

"Are you a poker-playing chap? I've thrown together a Monday-night poker game at the homestead. If you're interested, here's my address. 10:30 p.m. sharp—you know

William M. Brandon III

how poker players are: Nobody likes a late entry. Bad luck, you know?"

"Thanks. Perhaps I'll stop by. I'll talk to you later, Andy." As I walked out, I saw Andy sway in time to the washed-out love ballad on the overhead speakers. He was a good guy, but sometimes, I wondered.

As I walked back to my building, I noticed an eerie tension in a circle of hoodlums next to my building. I'd seen them around and they had seemed harmless, but I saw fear and anxiety in their eyes now. I looked up and one of the older boys was blocking my path. He had a switchblade in his right hand and it snapped open revealing a shiny four-inch blade.

"Alright man, here's where you cough up your wallet."

Anxiety was dripping from his tongue and the aroma of fear surrounded him like cheap cologne.

"I said, give me your fuckin' money." I stood there silently. He started moving the blade around in his hand. They were testing me. These kids were like trapped animals, and trapped animals must know their perimeters. They knew that one day, they would become trapped men unless they acted. Unfortunately, these boys thought crime was their ticket out. Petty crimes, but enough to get a kid from North Las Vegas permanently in the system. Now they had to know where I stood—the odd animal out. They had to know if they owned me through fear. The rest of my stay here depended on my reaction.

"The money I have in my wallet belongs to me. I would appreciate if you would let me pass."

"No chance, old-timer. Hand over the cash, now."

Old-timer? I was only twenty-five. I set my bag on the ground.

70

"I'm not giving you my wallet. End of story."

I had called his bluff, and now he had to react. The boy lunged toward me with the knife. I stepped to my left and caught his wrist. I grabbed him by the back of the neck and slammed his face against a wall. I held his face there and hit his hand against the bricks until he dropped the knife.

"God damn, you're slow. How old are you?"

"Fuck you." His voice strained from his face being forcibly pressed against brick.

I tightened my grip on his neck.

"What's your name?"

"Fuck you."

"So, let's talk. You are all invited to listen in," I gestured to the rest of the adolescents that they should gather 'round. "I want to live here without worrying that some punk kid is going to try to off me for the twenty dollars I have in my wallet. Is that too much to ask?"

I tightened my grip on his neck demanding an answer.

No one said a word.

"I'll take that as a 'yes.' I'm sure most of you haven't even lost your virginity yet, and believe me that's worth staying alive for. Leave me be to live my life and I promise not to pick you off one by one in the streets out of sheer boredom."

None of them spoke. Their pale, blank stares told me that I had either gotten through to them or that they were soiling their pants. I was satisfied with either outcome.

Those dumb-ass kids were brave, but they'd be dead before they saw eighteen.

Do You See Forever In Her Eyes?

I reached out to Gaelin after being buried in my own self-pity for more than a year.

We met at the Golden Gate Café.

"Man, you look like shit."

"Thanks, Gaelin. Is it the beard?"

"Sort of. It's more the gaunt face that the beard seems to be trying to hide. What's on your mind, Dean?" Gaelin seemed neither pleased nor upset to hear from me.

"A couple of things. First, I know you and Sarah are planning to leave Las Vegas in the fall. If this woman is what makes this world bearable for you, then I want this for you."

"You *know*? How do you know?"

"I followed you."

"Dean."

"I know. Hear me out."

"This time . . ."

"I know you two need a good start and as it turns out I need a new start as well."

Gaelin lowered his head, "Meaning?"

"Meaning a couple of my ex-crewmates ran into trouble in L.A. and one of them sold me out." Jake was dead, so Mike and Stretch went freelance and paid the price. Stretch went down without much of a fight. Mike shot a responding officer, was captured four blocks away, and was sitting in a holding cell detailing the whole sordid mess. "My accounts are frozen. I am destitute. Somehow, they haven't found me yet, but it's only a matter of time."

"What does this have to do with me?"

"One last job. To send you and Sarah off into the world without a care and to make me well again."

"I don't know . . . "

"It's easy money. Small bank, low traffic. They send for armored trucks every Tuesday. I have a third lined up, a pro. I'm driving and watching the door from the car. You just have to stand there looking menacing while our third bleeds the place dry."

"Maybe."

"I trust you. Besides, there's no one else," I added.

I invested no effort in hiding my agenda. I'd been where Gaelin thought he was. In that mystical land of numbness— of love—of proposed and accepted matrimony . . . head in the clouds . . . mind locked in silence unable to affect the outside world.

"Are you sure you want to do this with Sarah? Getting married and such?"

Love brings about emotive existence, a plane of reality foreign to the mind, a world with emotion as Parliament and the sex organs as Prime Minister.

"Sarah and I have been married for a month now. I wasn't sure you'd care to know. You're such a condescending bastard. I was afraid to hear all the negativity you were sure to spew at me. I know marriage isn't exactly your opinion of earthly bliss, Dean, but that doesn't necessarily mean that the institution itself is evil."

"It's not evil, it's all-consuming. Otherwise, why bother? Just make sure it's *everything*."

"You don't have to worry about us, Dean. Rest assured. Love cannot always be all-consuming, sometimes love is simply giving up what is holding you back."

"Holding you back from what?"

"Holding you back from being harmonious together." Gaelin looked me straight in the eye.

"That's rubbish. Does she love you or the condensed, newly equipped, aerodynamically styled, domesticated man she hopes she can mold you into?"

"Where are you getting all of this? I love Sarah, and I would do anything to make her happy."

"Then, do this job with me. A send off and a toast to forever." I pulled a cigarette from my pack and tucked it behind my ear. "I'll be back in five—think it over."

I knew how these things panned out: He'd give up anything to make her happy, but could she simply accept him as he his and be happy? Would she give that up for him? People will always be who they are. He can do everything in his power to be perfect for her, but he will still be who he is. He may be able to fight this his entire life, but it will manifest itself later. He'll become frustrated, short with Sarah, short with his beloved children; perhaps he'll fall prey to the idiocy of Mid-Life Crisis. If that happens, he'll be destroying Sarah's life, destroying his children's lives, and, most of all, he will wake up one day and realize that the last thirty years of his existence were a lie. This is what Gaelin should be thinking about. Not puppy dogs and picket fences but whether or not he can see forever in Sarah's eyes. If he can't, he must end it. She may still forgive him. Time destroys indiscriminately. If there exists a doubt in his mind, a weak link in Gaelin's love for Sarah, Time will devour both of them.

"Dean," Gaelin walked out onto the sidewalk. "I'll do it. Contact me about planning."

"Will do, Gaelin." I wanted to ask him . . . "Hey, what would you do with a glimpse at your future?"

"Change whatever I fucked up. Why?"

"Doesn't matter. See ya around."

§

I made my way to the back of the bar and used a payphone to call Gaelin.

"It's time."

"See you soon." Gaelin hung up.

I tripped over my feet while flipping a tip onto the bar. I had intended to leave several hours ago. Tempus fugit.

When I arrived at the Peppermill, Brown, an ex-con from Watts hired for the job, Gaelin, and Sarah were already getting antsy.

"What's shakin', kids?" I smiled calmly.

"Lookin' sharp, Dean." Brown was a sweet-talking con-man who took up robbing piggy banks after doing ten years for fraud.

"Thank you, sir. Much appreciated."

"Dean, this is Sarah," Gaelin gestured toward the soft–hued beauty to his right. Her long golden hair washed over her shoulders casually. She lacked the frailty of innocence and seemed a realistic bulwark against Gaelin's weary condescension. Her handshake was firm and her eyes never left mine.

"It's a pleasure, Dean."

"The pleasure is mine, Sarah," I slurred unconsciously.

"Want a drink to steady the nerves?" Brown offered as he signaled to their cocktail waitress.

"No, I'm steady as they go . . . come."

"You don't look steady," Sarah added.

"Look again, sister," I shot back.

"This seems like the time to instill confidence in your team." Sarah seemed hell-bent on attacking me. Probably on Gaelin's behalf. What awful things had he told her about me?

"Dean," Gaelin grabbed my arm, "are you drunk?"

"No." Yes.

"You've got to be kidding me. Sarah, we're out of here."

"I'll drive." There was no hint of fear in her voice.

"No way." Gaelin remained standing with his hands on the table.

"He's right, you're holding down the safe-house until Gaelin and I get back. You have to be the hub in case something goes wrong. No way."

"Thank you, Dean." Gaelin sat down.

"It's not a terrible idea. I mean, shit, with you concentrating on the door, everything will go a lot more smoothly, and we can always retrace our steps back to the hotel I have set up."

"I can do this." Sarah stared me down.

Gaelin's face twisted—this was a conversation she should be having with him. Instead, she was going toe to toe with me and I couldn't help but smile.

"Fine. Sarah's driving. We good?" I looked at Gaelin; this was his chance to call the whole thing off.

"Good." He relinquished his say on the matter.

"OK, let's go over the timing again. We'll leave here in," I checked my pocket watch, "thirty-three minutes. Brown will retrieve the car from the parking garage and pick us up from Boulder Station and head to the target . . . "

"Remember, there is only one entrance. I will be here at the door. If someone is going to enter, I'll escort them in and put them under Gaelin's careful control. Brown, you know what your job is. Do not stop for anything. Sarah will be here in eighty seconds, don't be late."

I paused.

"Are you ready?" I asked all around as we pulled to a stop in front of the US Bank on Flamingo.

"Yes," Gaelin answered immediately.

"Yeah," Brown chimed in, smiling.

"You bet," Sarah stared straight ahead and watched the flow of traffic.

"Then, let's go."

The sun scorched my neck's tender Gaelic flesh. The knot in my stomach was a familiar one. I watched Brown and Gaelin slide ebony sheathes over their faces and took my place outside the entrance to the bank. I lit a Pall Mall and carefully rolled the end with my tongue. Smooth as silk, drunk or not, I was on point.

There were some obscure people on the streets of Vegas that afternoon. Vegas' searing heat brings out stranger folks than Hollywood's full moons can boast. *Shit.* A woman walked directly toward me. Black sunglasses, cheap suit, and arrogance her bank account could not possibly afford. I lived for this sort of thing. I slid submissively to the side and, in a brief moment, as I swung the door open for her, she cast a flirtatious *thank you* before entering the bank. I ushered her in and, with one fluid motion, I pulled my 9mm, cocked it audibly, and pressed the barrel against the small of her back. She did not scream.

I tenderly told her to lay face first on the tile and remain quiet . . . please. Brown had already opened and emptied the appropriate drawers and files and was exiting the vault. Gaelin was stone cold and concentrated superbly on every individual in the bank.

"Five seconds," I called out. I stepped back into the intense heat. The streets warbled as the asphalt furnaces cooked the air, lending an underwater blur to all things farther than a hundred feet. The steady flow of sun-oppressed passers-by had ceased; Flamingo was dead silent.

Something felt wrong. I couldn't put my finger on it. *Maybe it's just the fact that it's 115 degrees right now. Better sharpen up just in case. Here comes Sarah, perfect.* Sarah was turning right off Howard Hughes Parkway. Brown and Gaelin walked calmly out of the front door while I covered them. Sarah pulled up as we reached the curb, and we stepped into the running vehicle. Gaelin, Sarah, and Brown started shouting and celebrating.

"Shut up, we're not out yet. Let's *try* to keep a low profile until we hit the spot," I barked.

"Lighten up, Dean. We pulled it off." Brown put his hand on my shoulder.

"How many gigs have you pulled? This makes three, right? Shut your mouth and keep your eyes open."

I felt it again. My stomach tensed; something was wrong. Sweet adrenaline flew in the breeze; the sour aroma of anticipation hung around it like a steel cage.

"Everyone put your seatbelts on and ready your sidearm."

"What's up, Dean?" Gaelin asked.

"I don't know, just strap up and be ready for anything."

Sarah looked briefly in the rear view mirror.

Maybe Gaelin was right. Right about Sarah. Maybe she was the complementary soul for his tortured existence. Maybe she could truly, finally make him happy. I hoped it all worked out . . .

"Dean," Sarah leaned toward me, "I think we're being followed—"

Crimson gushed from Sarah's neck and her life flooded onto my face and hands. Her head slumped against the wheel and her lifeless foot depressed the accelerator. I lunged across the seat and grabbed the wheel to steady the car. Gaelin was frozen in shock.

"Brown, undo my seatbelt!" I screamed to the back seat.

I was free.

I unlatched Sarah's restraint.

"Dean, no!" Gaelin reached forward to cradle his love; tears streamed down his face. I held him back as he tried to climb into the front seat. I was able to reach the door handle, and I watched in horror as I instinctively pushed Sarah's lifeless body out the door. She spun, reeling onto the asphalt and under the wheels of our pursuer's car. The car began to skid, slid across the opposing lane of traffic, and ran up and over a nearby parked car—hood-first through the front window of the Lime's Discount Mattress center.

"DEEEEEEEEEEEEAN—You fucking bastard! I'll kill you with my bare hands!" Gaelin lunged for my throat. Brown wrestled him down and pinned him as he kicked and thrashed.

"Brown, keep him down. I'm getting us out of here."

The car chasing us was a brown Crown Victoria, most likely an unmarked detective's car. Must have been on the block when the bank alarm call left dispatch. No one else appeared to be tailing us, least of all marked police cars. Sirens filled the air, but they were all headed to the bank. He must not have had time to call for backup or give a description of the car. It would be a matter of seconds before helicopters were airborne. I cleaned the blood off the windshield with my shirt and collected myself. After all, everyone in Vegas has a bullet hole in their car at one time or another.

I fish tailed into the parking structure of New York, New York and raced to the fourth level. I helped Brown drag Gaelin out of the backseat. Gaelin, barely able to stand, took several desperate swings and finally connected a fine right hook to my jaw. The pain wasn't physical—I knew he blamed me for Sarah—and tears welled up in my eyes as Gaelin collapsed to the ground sobbing.

"Gaelin, listen to me. We need to move, or we're dead men, period, end of story."

We walked as calmly as could be expected to the hotel entrance joining the fourth floor of the parking structure. Brown had a suite set up the night before where he was making himself visible with a couple of lady friends. When he opened the door, the ladies were still asleep.

"Perfect, they don't even know you left. Brown, get undressed and both of you, give me your guns."

Brown slid between the two prostitutes. Gaelin and I sat silently across from each other in the dining room; I lit a cigarette. Gaelin stared through the large windows surrounding the table. His rage had been overridden by a numb acceptance of futility.

"Gaelin, I'm sorry. It wasn't my idea to have her drive."

"Fuck you, Dean. This was *all* your idea. She shouldn't have been driving; she shouldn't have even been there. It was supposed to be you. You were supposed to take that bullet."

He was right. According to the newspaper article, I was supposed to die in that car.

"How do you know that?"

"She was never supposed to be there," he shouted, as if I were too dense to follow along.

The girls stirred.

Gaelin lowered his voice, "This was all for money. The one thing that has never brought either of us a stitch of happiness . . . ever. Cut me out—I don't want any part of it. I'm leaving; it's only a matter of time before they identify Sarah's body and start looking for me. She won't even get a proper burial."

"Gaelin, I think you should stay put for a while," I grabbed his arm.

"Dean, the rest of my days will be haunted with the question *what if?* This is what helplessness feels like—I completely understand you now." He pulled his arm away and slammed the door behind him.

"Ooh hello there, handsome." A gorgeous young woman barely wrapped in a sheet stood in the foyer—the epitome of a siren. Every curve of her flesh pricked desire in me. The way she stood sang volumes of sultry magnetism. Then, I looked into her eyes and saw nothing. Her pale eyes were dramatically shadowed by black. Some strokes by hand, some dedicated to years of late nights and cocaine brunch. Above her scarlet lips and windblown cheeks lay the cold blank stare of an actress who no longer believed in her role. Her movements were superb—rehearsed. She seemed to have lost her way playing the part—being something to everyone erodes sincerity. I learned the hard way that, in the end, the money can never be spent on happiness, only on controlling the pain.

"Where were you last night when I needed ya? Feel like finishing off what your friend Brown started?" she purred mechanically.

"No thanks, darlin'. You're off duty, have a seat."

"You're not some kind of *get to know me* John, are you?"

"No. Like I said, you're off the clock," I lit a cigarette for her. "Where are you from?"

"California."

"Where?"

"Why?"

I sat back and took a long drag from my cigarette.

"You don't have to answer. I'm just curious."

"Good."

We sat silently for the majority of my cigarette.

"I'm from Burbank. Born and raised," she recounted stoically. "And I bet I can answer the rest of your questions as well: I came from a good family, no one ever touched me growing up, I realized I could make a lot of money by doing something I did all the time anyway, so here I am. Anything else you want to know?"

"No, that clears everything up."

"You don't want me to pretend that I'm a good girl, just doing this to get through college? To finish my master's degree in chemistry? To feed my bastard kid or afford meth? A nice cheerleader type whose mother looked the other way while Daddy and assorted uncles scarred me for life with their immoral affections?"

"No. You've made your point," I conceded.

"Keep your pity to yourself, asshole."

I picked up my hat and made my way into the hall. I looked both ways, but Gaelin was really gone. Gone for good. I whispered *goodbye* under my breath and headed for the elevator.

I walked down the street feeling the weight of the world resting squarely on my shoulders. I slid into the joint I had frequented a year ago and sat down to drink myself into oblivion. I laid a $100 bill on the bar and instructed the barkeep that it was his under two conditions:

"Leave me completely alone. When I signal for you, pour me your finest whiskey, and then refer to condition number one."

He accepted, and I brought the glass to my lips. I could smell my salvation in its intoxicating vapors. Heat overtook me as my blood rushed to my head, thirsting, craving for the numbing medicine. I tilted the glass, but before I could appease my blood's craving I saw something in the mirror behind the bar—ebony curls and burning emerald eyes. There she was, my angel with Wilde on her lips and flame in her eyes.

After Selene, after all that had happened, this woman walked back into my reality. It could not be blind coincidence, and fate was a bedtime story for infant charlatans and the pounders of pulpits. No, there was no reason for her to interrupt my life, but I would not let her slip by me again. It was time to let go of Selene. It was time to face the fact that she and I were separated by powers outside of our control, and no matter how much I loved her, no matter how much she loved me, we could never reclaim what once was. My memory of her was so vibrant; she was so beautiful, so utterly disgusted with the banality of this universe. I reached out to kiss her delicate cheek . . .

"Goodbye, Selene."

I had to move along with life and kill my memory of Her. I had to try to love another as I had Selene, or accept the wretched fact that I might die alone. I could not accept this lying down—I had to try to alter fate, I had to try to control destiny, I had to try to see forever . . .

. . . in Her eyes.

Faith Asunder

It's dangerous to put your dreams into tangible forms. It leaves them open to be ripped asunder. Dreams are best kept in the deepest recesses of the mind. Danger is afoot when you allow these feelings and emotions into the light of day. I knew better than to allow myself to be hurt like this, but I truly thought that this was *it*, and to realize that it was over tore at my heart with Herculean strength.

I saw her that night: The dove that threatened to glide through my dreams and ravish my desires. I was on the same stool I had barely been able to wrestle into a proper seat on the night I first saw her. Now, however, I had my wits about me. I was drunk, but my intoxication was borne of the silken touch of her skin, the majesty of her porcelain neck, the erotic curve of her lower back, and the penetrating fires of her emerald eyes. *This time, I will not lose her.* A need I could not subdue screamed to me: *Your salvation lies in this woman's gossamer caress.*

Well, when your subconscious is screaming such poetry, it's difficult to combat it with logic. (Hell, I don't even try anymore.) I parted my lips to prevent her from walking right past me, and anxiety thrust through my mid-section with sound-barrier-breaking force. I pulled back within myself and resolved to give up again. Anxiety was an omnipotent force that governs my every move.

No, not this time. Perhaps she was all I needed to complete myself (or I would be able to convince myself of this), and I'd be damned if my personal inadequacies would banish me into eternal love of my addictions. I stood up, adjusted my thoughts (and my tie), and strode across the bar to where she was sitting, delicately sipping a glass of blood-red wine with a gentleman. I glared fiercely and lovingly into her eyes and held out my hand. She took my hand and seemed not to hear her gentleman friend's protests. I stared into this man's eyes fiercely. The threat of violence instilled in him a sense that this was of no concern to him, and his best option was to sit down quietly and try to forget that this angel had ever touched his life.

We danced through the streets of Las Vegas discussing our decaying society and finally resolved that neither of us felt the ability nor the responsibility to solve the world's problems when the neon turned the night into day and an entire city lay in wait.

I stroked her sun-kissed cheek and tucked a straying ebony curl behind her ear with a tenderness that surprised us both. Our eyes locked and the entire world around us with its poisonous automobiles and deadly neon, its serial killers and rapists of children, its cold, cold depression, temporarily existed outside of our gaze. Instinctively, our lips met. The perfect marriage of passion and gentleness.

I don't know how long we kissed, but when she pulled her lips from mine, I longed to wrap my arms around her and keep the union forever. I was again locked in her hypnotic gaze as she traced my lips with her fingers as if allowing the rest of her skin to feel the passion her lips had just experienced. She looked longingly into my eyes and said, "Take me away from here. I give myself to you completely."

We sped to her home nestled forcefully at the base of our lovely western mountain range. The view from her veranda was breathtaking, but I could not separate my eyes from hers, despite the fact that sipping precious Sapphire without the aid of one's eyes requires more motor skills than I have ever claimed to possess.

"This feeling must have a tangible reference, or I will always be tortured as to whether or not you are a reality," I said, touching her hand.

"The one thing you need to know is that I need you tonight," she responded. "Your eyes, your menacing hands, the sweet smell of spent tobacco on your collar. I want you desperately—all else is of little consequence."

I cradled her body in my arms and laid her down on a breathtaking four-poster berth draped with diaphanous silk and mind-numbing burgundy velvet. My senses reeled as I felt her tender fingertips running down my arms, tracing the muscles in my back and stomach. The way she touched me made me weep for those who have never felt the caress of a woman who will always and forever excite and stimulate. As she stared into my eyes and whispered words I could never defile by writing, I carefully touched my lips to her neck, covering every inch of this goddess's intoxicating flesh with my mouth. Her increasingly heavy breathing told me volumes of the pleasures she knew I could make her feel, and my will solidified into that singular obsession. She arched her back in ecstasy as I parted her blouse and lovingly caressed her skin with the edge of my lips, feeling her heart thrust against my skin and awaken every nerve in my countenance. She tore hungrily at my shirt until I removed it.

The sensuality of her touch erased the world around me and all of my concentration and strength became engulfed in making this woman sigh and moan and grope in ecstasy that she could not control. Control was of no concern. Control was the last thought that could dance through our minds. The flood was all consuming; even the symbiotic movement of our hips as this consummation took place seemed to naturally occur to the end of sending her into waves upon waves of sensual release. She gripped my shoulders and rolled violently into a position of dominance. She looked down at me with an obsequious smile as her subtle hips moved pendulum-like over mine. God, I could feel her. I could feel her tense as the waves of ecstasy rolled through her body again and again with infinitely more intensity. I placed my hands firmly on her hips and continued this motion for her. She relaxed her legs as I moved her back and forth against my body, and she felt her release without the constraints of movement. The volume and intensity of her climax rippled through my body and made it impossible to subdue mine any longer. We thrust against one another, thrashing to keep the moment alive, neither one of us willing to let go of this purifying flood of erotic seizure. Finally, she slumped over, wet with the perspiration of a thousand blistering desert nights, and lay exhausted by my side. As I stroked her hair, I felt that this was where she should stay for all time.

I got up to retrieve a cigarette for her. The blank, exhausted look on her face surprised me. A strange frigid wind slid across my flesh. I shuddered. I lit one for both of us and laid my head on her lap as we both breathed in the carcinogens with a slow, calculated intensity. Jennifer stroked my hair and I was lost in my thoughts. When she spoke, I was startled.

"Do you want me to call a cab, darlin'?"

I could barely hear what she was saying over my own labored breath.

"Cab?"

"You didn't drive," she stated flatly.

"Right. Certainly. I'll call after this," I pointed to my burning cigarette and leaned in to kiss her exposed neck.

"Come on, we've already been over all of that." She shirked away from my kiss and though she had a playful smile on her face, her words cut deeply.

"Yes, but once is never enough," I tried to regain ground.

"You should leave." She was not amused.

"I'm sorry, I didn't mean to offend . . . "

"I think you should leave. Now."

I couldn't believe what I was hearing.

"Please don't look at me like that. This isn't love. This isn't forever. We just shared something amazing—let's not ruin it with premature sentimentality."

It became clear to me that the man she was with at the bar could just as easily have ended up in her bed tonight. I had held a renewed sense of hope, and now, it was being ripped from my hands. This ethereal two hours of pleasure had truly been pure lust and nothing else. I had defiled Selene's memory for naught.

"That's it? Am I never to see you again?" I stammered.

"I'm a married woman. Happily married, if you can believe it . . . " she smiled tiredly and kissed my cheek. " I can see that this meant more to you than it did to me, so I think it would be better if we didn't see each other again. Why ruin it? We had a lovely time that I fear may never be duplicated, but it does not constitute love. I don't mean to be cruel, but it would be far crueler to lie to you about how I felt. I think you should go."

I was barely able to stand as pain, not physical but emotional, shot through my every nerve, peaking finally with a vengeance in my heart. I staggered a bit. Then, it struck me. My ever-powerful, ever-present defense mechanisms kicked in. I would not let myself feel this way. Not now, never.

I gave the driver my address but never made it. I asked him to stop at Circus Circus and I stumbled down the strip moving in and out of lounges until the neon reds, yellows, and whites sent me reeling into a gutter behind Harrah's. I never saw Jennifer again, and it's probably better that way. My love belonged to only one woman and I lost her forever to the swirling waters of time.

Here I sit with my addictions.

The truest, dearest, most understanding, and steadfast friends I have ever known. They were also probably my ultimate demise. I lost my final delusion that night. Trust was dead, faith was crippled, and optimism seemed too grand an ideal. I'd lost faith in my own humanity, but that's to be expected in this day and age.

The end.

Special thanks to: Kevin Staniec, Marisa Roemer, Elise Portale, Ashley Heaton, Davide Bonazzi, Corrie Greathouse, William S. Burroughs.

William recently relocated to breathtaking and traffic-free Athens, Georgia, from back-breaking and happiness-eviscerating Los Angeles, California. He began his lifelong roadtrip in the deprecated sands of Las Vegas, Nevada, and as a result of a military patriarch, and a subsequent unabated restlessness, has changed addresses fifty-six times in thirty-eight years. These days he earns his pittance from a real-life Kafkan nightmare and daydreams about sitting behind his typewriter working on his fifth novel, playing the drums in a project that is disrespectful of homogenous time signatures, and conversing with his astonishing wife and his brilliant six-year-old stepson.

William's synaptic meanderings have appeared on his website (agentofdiscord.com), in technical form on WIRED.com and THALO.com, in memoir/novel form in A Selfish Man (Publish America – 2003), in short story form in Rain Crow Magazine (Athens Diptych – Issue #2), will appear again next year in short story form in an anthology supporting the non-profit Mines Advisory Group (The Atlantic – 2013), and finally, in voluminous letters to persons still enchanted with non-electronic communication. PS they almost never write back…

Elise Portale is an always editor and sometimes writer with a degree in Creative Writing from Chapman University. During the day, she is mild-mannered managing editor for such national publications as *American Survival Guide* and *Gun World* and has contributed to *Romantic Homes*, *Flea Market Décor*, and many others. When she's not cleaning up copy, Elise jumps around Orange County looking for all things musical, visual, literary, and culinary to inspire her.

Davide Bonazzi lives in Bologna (Italy), where he was born in 1984. After he graduated from the University of Bologna, Faculty of Arts and Humanities, he studied Illustration in Milan at IED – European Institute of Design and at the Academy of Fine Arts of Bologna. Since 2008 he works as a freelance illustrator. Among his clients, *The Boston Globe*, *The Wall Street Journal*, *Scientific American*, *Columbia Magazine*, Hachette Books, Timberland, Greenpeace, L'Espresso and many others.